M. Jones

The Story of Edward the Black Prince

M. Jones

The Story of Edward the Black Prince

ISBN/EAN: 9783744749893

Printed in Europe, USA, Canada, Australia, Japan

Cover: Foto ©Andreas Hilbeck / pixelio.de

More available books at **www.hansebooks.com**

THE TILTING MATCH.

Page 113

THE

STORY OF EDWARD

THE BLACK PRINCE.

BY

M. Jones.

With Illustrations.

"I'll tell you a tale of a knight, my boy;
The bravest that ever was seen."

London:

T. NELSON AND SONS, PATERNOSTER ROW.

EDINBURGH; AND NEW YORK.

1883.

Preface.

THE wars of Edward III. in France are sometimes spoken of as though they were mere wars of aggression. To this view of them I cannot give an unqualified assent. The law of succession, though pretty well ascertained, was not so strictly observed in those days as to prevent all controversy upon the subject. And seeing that, in his peculiar case, others, beside Edward himself, thought that he had a claim to the crown of France, I am disposed to look upon his French wars as springing from an honest determination on his own part, and that of his people, to rectify, by force the wrong which, as he conceived, had been done him by the French nobles, in assigning the throne to Philip of Valois.

I do not affirm that he was in the right; but

I do think he had sufficient grounds for supposing himself to be so. The circumstances of the case were undoubtedly such as to leave room for honest difference of opinion about it. Nor do I think that any one of us, who had as colourable a claim to a great estate as had Edward III. to the French crown, would leave any stone unturned in our efforts to get possession of it. Of course we should not fight; that is the ultimate process of nations. But not a single law court should we leave unvisited, carrying up our appeal step by step, until we gained our cause, or were barred by the final adverse decision of the highest court of all: as Edward was ultimately barred by the final adverse decision, unmistakeably expressed by successes in arms, of the French nation.

Much, however, as men may differ as to the merits of his claim, all must unite in unbounded admiration of the courage, fortitude, judgment, and generosity, displayed by our great monarch, and his greater son, in those marvellous encounters between the few and the many, which have, for five long centuries, made Crecy and Poitiers names of pride throughout England. And the present seems a peculiarly suitable time for recalling in detail the far-off glories of the two Edwards; seeing that "wars and rumours of wars" have, since 1854, been almost incessantly around us; and we, the *few*, as we were on those old battle-fields, are sometimes disposed to look anxiously upon the *many* that, as we apprehend, may be against us. But Norman fire, grafted upon Anglo-Saxon endurance, is still our inheritance; and should war, either at home or abroad, be thrust upon us,—with a just cause, and, above all, with "God" for "our Hope and Strength," we may with confidence look to come out of it as triumphantly as did the little imperiled band that followed Edward into France, and with more permanence of success than was awarded to them.

Englishmen still pray, as well as fight!

M. J.

LONDON, *September* 11, 1863.

Contents.

List of Illustrations.

The Childhood of the Black Prince.

HE French wars of our great Edward III., and his greater son, Edward the Black Prince, afford a wonderful example of what stout English hearts and hands can achieve, even in the face of overwhelming numbers. Those wars have made Creçy and Poitiers household words in England, and we now propose to tell, in detail, their story; together with that of the gallant leader under whom the English name became terrible in France. We shall find the narrative present us with admirable pictures of fortitude, humanity, and generosity, as well as of warlike skill and daring.

Edward, the Black Prince, the heroic son of Edward III. of England, was born at the old royal palace of Woodstock, on the 15th of June, 1330. His mother was Philippa, daughter of William, Count of Hainault. In 1327, when she was a mere girl of fourteen, the princess, attended by a brilliant train of knights

and gentlemen, came over to England to marry its
young monarch, who was only two or three months
older than herself.   The marriage proved a happy one;
more so than usually falls to the lot of royal personages: for Philippa was gentle and good, and sincerely
attached to her husband; and he, in return, gave her,
throughout their long life, the affection she so well
deserved.   The birth of their boy was a great delight
both to them and the whole nation; and in the glad-
ness of his heart the king munificently rewarded the
bearer of such welcome tidings, assigning him a liberal
yearly pension in money, till he could settle lands
upon him to the same value.

We do not know much about the royal nursery in
those days.   One thing, however, we *do* know, that the
first year or two in that apartment are spent very
much alike, whatever may be the centuries compared.
Whether the date be 1800 or 1300,—kicking, crawling,
squalling, and eating porridge, equally engrosses the
young occupant, be he prince or be he peasant.   This
may not be very dignified, but we cannot help that.
The further process of shortening those interminable
long tails to their petticoats, with which it is the custom to endow very young babies, also passes upon a
Prince of Wales, irrespective of the date of his birth.
While in his first attempts to walk, the tumbles and
knocks upon the head, encountered by the heir-apparent
of our day, have certainly been shared by that stalwart

child whom we see so dimly through the mist of five receding centuries.   For both, the same mother's heart has beaten; and, tender as was that of Philippa for her first-born, we may not believe that it was more tender than that of her whom we English of this day love to call our sovereign.

One would certainly have liked to know something of the childhood of one who was destined to fill so important a part in our own history, and in that of our neighbours across the channel, as does the Black Prince.   But though we have gossip five centuries old, it is not gossip about babies.   For grave historians to record that Joan of Oxford was his nurse; that Mistress Matilda Frampton had the honour of rocking the royal cradle; and that, in his third year, he was created Earl of Chester; is not telling us much : it is the boy himself we want to hear about.   But the nursery door is close shut upon its little princely inmate, and however precocious or stupid he may have been, to us it is all a blank.

At the age of six, however, we get a glimpse of our Edward of the olden time; for his father then created him Duke of Cornwall, a title that is still borne by the Prince of Wales.   In those days, the creation of a peer was a ceremony; not as now, when a slip of paper converts a banker into a lord ; and the ceremony, in this case, must have been a sight worth seeing.   A title meant something then.   It carried with it power and authority, and the symbols of these were formally delivered to him who received it. Perhaps it was because the prince was such a very little fellow that all the usual formalities were not gone through on this occasion. His rights over the duchy of Cornwall were, ceremoniously, conveyed to him simply by girding his tiny waist with a sword; the other usual ensigns of authority—the ring and the staff—were not transferred to him. The new-made duke, the first that England had ever known, immediately proceeded to show that the distinction conferred upon him was no empty one. Bestowing knighthood was one of the powers attached to it, and twenty gallant youths that day received it from his hand. By this time, too, we find that the small man was minding his book, with grave Dr. Burley for his tutor, and a group of youngsters to learn lessons with him, instead of being left in stately solitude to con them over by himself. Among these associates, Simon Burley afterwards became one of the prince's favoured and most distinguished knights.

King Edward's French wars, of which we shall speak presently, carried him much abroad; and his Highness of Cornwall (he was not Prince of Wales yet), was, in his father's absence, appointed Lieutenant of the kingdom. His lieutenancy was no mere pretence, not a name only; for this child of eight years old actually held a parliament for his father at Northamp-

ton, in 1338.   A most obliging parliament it was too;
for, under the young duke's presidency, it voted large
supplies for carrying on the popular war with Philip
of Valois and his friends.

Here, again, those tiresome old chroniclers do not
tell us how the prince got through his important business, nor even how much of it fell to his share.   But
at the mature age of eight, he would certainly get on
better than did James VI. of Scotland, who, (at three
or four years old), having to perform a regal duty of
the same kind, wound up his address to Lords and
Commons, by remarking, in the same breath, that
there was a hole in the roof of the parliament-
house.   We cannot for one moment suppose that
our Edward made such "a hole" in his manners as
this !

The promise of the young prince's babyhood—for he
really was a fine child—was now being fulfilled.   He
grew up a handsome, strong-limbed, intelligent lad ;
and at the age of nine, when his father, who was busy
preparing for his contest with the French, sent for him
to the castle of Louvain to keep Christmas with himself and his queen, one of the Christmas amusements
of that "noble and royal" assembly was to propose a
marriage between the boy and the little daughter of
the Duke of Brabant, the young lady being then four
years old.   The match went no further than those
Christmas conversations by a blazing log-fire; one of

the prince's own countrywomen, celebrated for her
beauty as the "Fair Maid of Kent," being destined
for the wife, not of a hopeful boy, but of a man renowned throughout Christendom as the hero of Crecy,
Poitiers, and Najar.

Origin of the Wars in France.

T the time that King Edward III. came to the throne, the English had considerable possessions in the south of France, which had been brought by Queen Eleanor, wife of Henry II., as her marriage portion. For these possessions the kings of England had been accustomed to do homage to the kings of France, as (what was called) their *feudal* superiors. This ceremony did not at all affect their independence as sovereigns of England. It only related to their lordship over those French duchies, in relation to which they were not quite so supreme as was the monarch of France, and as they themselves were at home: they owed to the French king, so far as these French dominions were concerned, a limited sort of obedience, in compliance with what was called the feudal law.

The feudal system, of which this law was a part, was a relic of the old conquering times when he who had won lands by his sword—as William the Norman did in England—portioned them out among his followers, on condition that their swords should help him in case of need: the amount of military service, thus rendered, being in proportion to the extent of lands bestowed.   Other independent sovereigns, besides those of England, though none of such importance and grandeur as they, were in the same position as Edward: owning feudal obedience to some one who, in that particular, was greater than they.   But, saving this mere feudal obedience, it would not have been wise for any feudal lord, however high and mighty, to require more from them.   In such a case, they would have flown in the face even of his Highness of France as readily as in that of a meaner potentate.

This sort of feudal obedience, then, had been rendered by our monarchs, on account of their portion of the kingdom of France.   But on the death of Charles the Fair, King of France, in 1328, our Edward III., as his nephew, considered that he was the next heir to the throne, and therefore, as supreme lord, had a right to the whole kingdom.   The great lords and peers of France thought otherwise, and gave the crown to Philip of Valois, cousin to the late king.   Their reason for preferring a more distant relation than Edward, was that as (according to the custom of France, which does not suffer a woman to reign), Queen Isabella of England could not succeed to the crown herself, neither could her son inherit through her.   Edward and his friends were, however, confident in their view of the case. Indeed, there was room for dispute in the matter; and most probably the real reason why Philip was chosen instead of Edward, was, not so much out of regard to the Salic law, as to the circumstance of Philip's being a Frenchman, one of themselves, while Edward was an English king.

There was only one way of deciding such a quarrel, that is, by fighting; and to this the English king, with the hearty concurrence of his people, and the purchased help of his allies, speedily resorted.

Believing himself to be the rightful heir to the French throne, it was not particularly agreeable to Edward, in the first flush of youth and sovereignty, to be called upon to go over to France, and perform that customary homage of which we have been speaking, for a mere corner of the kingdom. The whole belonged to him, as he thought; why then should he go down upon his knees to return thanks for the limited ownership of a part of it? King Philip had already been crowned a twelvemonth, and all his other feudatories—as those who acknowledged him for feudal superior, were called—had done homage to their lord in the manner prescribed. The mode of doing this was for the feudatory or vassal, to kneel bareheaded, unbelted, and unarmed before his lord, between whose hands he placed his own, vowing the customary obedience; or, in other and old words, promising

to become his " man." The lord then bestowed a
kiss upon the kneeling knight, and the ceremony was
at an end.

It was, as has been said, excessively disagreeable to
Edward, as King of England, thus to humble himself
to his neighbour.   Young as he was (he was only seventeen), he was already distinguished, not only as sovereign of a realm that might vie in importance with
that of France, but for the energy and valour which he
had displayed in his contests with the fierce, rude
warriors of Scotland.   And his high spirit, high both
from his position, and from his personal merit, revolted from the ceremonial submissiveness required
from him.   According to the custom of that age, however, he could not absolutely refuse it when summoned,
unless he had been prepared at once to go to war
about the matter.

Accordingly, when Philip's messengers requiring the
accustomed duty from the English king, presented
themselves at Windsor,—which had, even then, for
more than two centuries been a royal palace,—they
were received with all the courtesy due to their own
rank, and that of their master.   But, with the same
punctilious politeness, they were informed that the
king must consult with his council, before he could
engage to perform the homage demanded from him.
Edward forthwith came up to town, and assembled
his trusty councillors at Westminster.   Before them

the messengers laid their credentials, and then withdrew, while the knotty question, to pay homage or
refuse it—in other words, peace or war—was discussed.
Discretion is said to be the better part of valour, and
the council possessed this valuable quality; for, seeing
that the nation was not, just then, in a condition to back
their king, with "bills and bows," if he declined compliance with the French king's demands, they decided
that he should obey Philip's bidding. The messengers
were then again summoned before that stately assem-
blage; and by the mouth of the Bishop of London (in
those days bishops were often leading statesmen), were
duly informed that the king, their master, would forthwith pass over into France to render the homage required by his cousin Philip.

So far all seemed smooth. Edward kept his word,
and on the 26th of May 1329, set out on this unpleasant errand, attended by a fitting train of nobles,
bishops, and knights. His suite comprised a thousand
horse, and he was received by Philip, with correspond-
ing magnificence, at Amiens; where the homage was
paid in presence of three kings—those of Bohemia,
Navarre, and Majorca, and a crowd of nobles, drawn
together to do honour to the new liegeman. Never
was bitter pill more brightly gilded. But it *was* a
bitter pill, that Edward at first made some difficulty
about swallowing in the prescribed fashion. He made
his appearance in the Cathedral of Amiens (where his

"lord" sat in a .chair of state), armed and royally robed; nor was he disposed either to strip himself of his regal and knightly insignia, or to do the kneeling part of the business. Both, however, were relentlessly exacted of him; and, in a terrible temper, Edward of England, avowed himself vassal—for Guienne—to Philip of France; whom, in his secret soul, he wished at Jericho.* Fifteen days were afterwards passed in feasting, tournaments, and grave conferences, between the politicians of that brilliant congress; and then Edward returned to his young wife at Windsor, well pleased with his reception at the French court, however much he might dislike that part of the performance in which he had been the leading actor.

Among the nobles of France who had assisted in placing the crown upon the head of Philip of Valois, was his brother-in-law, Count Robert of Artois. He was a particularly great man, and stood so high in Philip's good graces, that almost everything in the kingdom was guided and ordered by my Lord Robert. Ere long, however, Philip's violent liking for his brother-in-law turned, as is not uncommon, to an equally violent hatred of him. The count's moral character was certainly nothing to boast of. Indeed, it is said that he was guilty of the shabby vice of forging title deeds, in order to mend his claim on certain lands in France.

---

* It has been denied that Edward performed his homage in the humiliating manner described. But some old authorities take this view of it.

On account of this, Philip was strongly inclined to cut off the count's head, if he could only catch him! and after having hunted his intended victim out of several states, to which, in succession, he had fled from the axe and block prepared for him, Robert was at last fairly driven to England, for the shelter denied him elsewhere.

Philip had much better have let his brother-in-law stay quietly at home, and keep his cunning head on his broad shoulders; for, once in the court of England, he diligently employed all the influence which a man of his reputation possessed, in urging upon the king the justice of his claim to the French throne, and in inciting that young, valorous spirit to plead his cause with the sword. Such a mode of upholding it could not but be agreeable to one yet glowing with successful fight against those, over whom his grandfather had so long ridden, rough-shod, that he began at last to think he really had a right to do it. The Frenchman accompanied Edward in his expedition against the Scots, and while in the field plied him well with arguments for flying at higher game. He further comforted the soul of the young monarch by assuring him that his claim was held good by several lawyers.

Count Robert was reckoned a man of great sagacity. He was also of royal descent. No wonder that the king began at last to yield to his persuasions, and to hold many anxious conferences with his council, as to whether he should, or should not, carry his steel-clad host from the bare heaths of Scotland, which they had already trampled down, to try their fortune on the fair fields of France. The knights of those days, be it said, rather preferred fighting in France, to fighting in Scotland; as the former country afforded them more luxurious quarters.

Edward's council were well enough disposed that the king should advance his claim to the French crown, and prosecute it by arms, if need were. The resources of his own kingdom were not, however, at the time adequate to do this; and to do it effectually he must seek aid from his friends and allies on the continent. They, therefore, advised that he should send ambassadors to his gallant and gouty father-in-law, the Earl of Hainault, to ascertain what could be done in that quarter. To these ambassadors, the earl and his brother, the Lord John, gave all that was in their power to give, that is, advice; a very good thing when nothing better is to be had. And acting upon their counsel, Edward contracted alliances with the lords, and small sovereigns of the Low Countries; who, some for love, more for money, and others, won by the cheaper means of flattery and promises, agreed to aid him in his grand enterprise.

One of Edward's allies in this business was, it is true, neither sovereign nor lord, though he was as powerful and important as though he were both the one and the other. This ally was Jacob van Arteveld, who, having retired from the brewing business, which he had carried on with great success, next took up that of governing the Flemings, in a style rather more imperative than had ever been adopted by their lawful sovereign, the Earl of Flanders. From the earl they had thought proper to revolt; but whether they liked the brewer any better, after they had got him, may be questioned, for Jacob had an awkward habit of killing off, without the slightest ceremony, any one to whom it pleased him to take a dislike. Further, as is frequently the case, when men of low birth are raised to power and wealth, he was much more extragavant— with the money of the Flemings—than the earl had ever been, who was born to these two good things. He taxed the Flemings heavily in a variety of ways. They had both indirect, and direct, exceedingly direct, taxation; for after he had spent the accustomed duties, no one knew, nor dared to ask, how, he would proceed to what *he* called borrowing large sums from the citizens; his borrowing, being the next best, or worst thing to demanding, seeing that no one who had any regard for his own safety, felt at liberty to say—no! Indeed, whenever he thought fit to tell them he wanted more money, it was always best to take his word for it, and let him have it. In short, Jacob played King Stork among his new subjects with a vengeance!

To this amiable individual King Edward addressed

himself so effectually, that the stout, sturdy Flemings, fat-
tened and strengthened on such beer as Jacob had been
wont to brew, were joined in his cause, with the more
sprightly cavaliers of the empire; that is, of Austria
and Germany.   When Edward's own forces were united
to these, there was a gallant army under his direction,
or that of his lieutenants, who, with various fortune,
kept fighting a little here, and a little there, for the next
eight years.   Amid their skirmishing we may notice
that Count Robert came to his end; and finally found
a quiet resting-place in the choir of our old St. Paul's.
The din of the city, teeming with mercantile life, per-
chance even now roars around the ashes of that turbulent warrior.   His death was lamented in England, for
he had qualities to win admiration in those far off days;
and according to the fashion (more heathen than Christian), of the times, Edward swore to take a terrible revenge for it.

Towards the close of this period of skirmishing, that
is in 1343, when the young Edward was thirteen years
old, his father, with all solemnity, conferred upon him
the title of Prince of Wales.   The king also thought
that with the help of Jacob the brewer, the revolted
Flemings might be persuaded to accept the young prince
as their sovereign.   But the earldom of Flanders was
not to be added to the rest of his titles and possessions.
Van Arteveld was heartily willing to do all that Edward
wished from him.   It was very pleasant to patronize a

king. But he soon found that he had promised more than he could perform. He condescended to consult with his turbulent Flemings, on the question of this contemplated transfer of their allegiance; but it seems that by this time they were tired of Jacob and his iron rule. They murmured loudly at the proposal, declaring that, with God's help, they would never disgrace themselves so far as to disinherit their "natural lord, in favour of a stranger." And they whispered, one to another, that Jacob was carrying things with rather too high a hand; and they would not endure it any longer. Nor did they; for forthwith the mob fell upon the unfortunate brewer, and killed him.

Edward, who, attended by the prince, and a stately retinue, had come over to Sluys in Flanders, and was there anxiously awaiting the result of Jacob's negotiations, was not easily pacified after this destruction of his hopes. He immediately took his son home again, vowing vengeance against the Flemings, and all belonging to them. Those discreet people, however, soon patched up a peace with him; and though they begged to be excused from any attempt to deprive their young Earl Lewis of his rights, they adroitly insinuated that, as the king had a daughter, Flanders might very possibly be ruled by his family after all, through her marriage with their lord.

And so the poor brewer, whose mangled remains were scarcely cold in their unhonoured grave, was forgotten as speedily as possible, and every one was quite comfortable.

Jacob's fate was sad; but his violence had merited it. He had taken "the sword," and he "perished" by it.

Passage of the Somme.

EDWARD'S disappointment at the loss of the earldom of Flanders, which he had hoped to secure for his son, was not merely for the loss of title and territory. We know how he longed to gain possession of what he considered his rightful inheritance; how this longing had led him to court the brewer of Ghent; and might have induced him to cultivate even more ignoble acquaintance, could they have served him in the matter. The reason for his wish to gain the Flemings was his having entertained the hope of making Flanders his key to unlock that beautiful, fertile France, out of which (with the exception of his own hereditary portion) he was kept, as he thought, so unjustly. And now that roaring raging mob in the peaked and gabled streets of Ghent, had put an end to his fine scheme. But for this, it is to be feared that the slaughter of a dozen brewers, instead of only one, would not have disturbed his tranquillity.

But there were other roads into France besides those

through Flanders, and King Edward was soon to find them. For two years or more his lieutenants in the south of France, where he was "at home," and no one denied it, had been as busy as possible in dealing out hard knocks to their neighbours—the less loved that they were such near neighbours. His cousin, the Earl of Derby, (not of the house of Stanley, but a royal Plantagenet), was driving all before him in Gascony, where he had met with little opposition; for to carry on war successfully requires plenty of money; and money was just the thing that Philip of Valois wanted. In the early part of 1346, however, Philip contrived to get so far out of his difficulties as to raise an army of a hundred thousand men, who, with lords and knights almost innumerable, marched into Gascony, under the command of the Duke of Normandy, and set themselves, so steadily, and successfully, to the retaking of the Earl of Derby's conquests in that province, that the thing soon became serious. Sir Walter Manny, who had, a few years before, come over to England in the train of the good Queen Philippa, was with the comparatively small body of English who were thus fiercely attacked in southern France; and though he was in himself a host, his skill and bravery, with that of other knights, also brave and skilful, did not prevent the fortune of war from going sadly against them.

In this strait Edward proposed going himself to the assistance of his faithful, but harassed followers. His people heartily seconded him. Men and arms, and ships for their transport, were soon collected, and the young prince, now in his sixteenth year, was to have his first experience of actual war among them.

Masses of soldiers, armed and accoutred for their deadly, though necessary function, form a picturesque spectacle even in our own days. But, in comparison with the very olden time of which we are writing, war is now shorn of almost all its strange, outside beauty. There were the knights glittering in plate armour, helmeted, crested, plumed, with each one his bright shield, throwing off sunbeams as he moved along; while their satin and embroidered surcoats were fit for the train of a duchess on drawing-room days. The surcoat was a flowing sort of robe, thrown over the armour. The lance, with its little fluttering pennon, was an exceedingly picturesque weapon, as we may see by our modern lancers. Nor was the huge steel battle axe, or hammer, (*martel*, was its old name,) added by some to the ordinary equipment of lance and sword, and which was slung from their saddle-bow, other than an imposing looking implement of destruction.

Then the horses were nearly as fine, and well defended by plates of steel, as their masters. How puzzled the poor animals must have felt, to be stalking about in iron cases; and further, on high days and holidays, with what one may call embroidered petticoats down to their heels!

(3)

3

The man-at-arms—what we should now call the cavalry soldier—though less brilliantly mailed than the knight or noble, was not the less encased in good serviceable metal, that would withstand sword stroke, or spear-thrust. Indeed, we are told that prostrate knights and men-at-arms, defying all penetrating weapons, have had to be cracked like lobsters, by blows of the hammer, before the death-dealing dagger could find its way through their iron shells.

This man-at-arms with his little retinue of attendants (for he was a great man in his way), formed a striking group; while the mounted and mail-clad host were varied by bodies of archers, in their loose, easy-fitting dress: for we did not, in those days, strap and buckle up our soldiers as we do now. These stout fellows were armed with the formidable bow and arrow of our old English yeomen: bows as tall as themselves, wherein the yard-long shaft was drawn by main strength of body, not of arms merely, right up to the ear, before it was discharged on its twanging, death-carrying errand. Those yard-long arrows would pierce the stoutest armour impervious to all ordinary weapons. As for our Irish and Welsh fellow subjects, who now hold their own in our armies as well as the best of us, making men proud to enter their distinctive regiments; they did not come out at all well in the days of Edward III. and our wars in France. In fact they were a long way behind the English in civilization; so a big knife, or any other awkward tool that was capable of doing mischief, was thought quite good enough for them.

"Tell that" *not* "to the marines," but to the Welsh Fusiliers, and Connaught Rangers.

Of such was the small though effective army now destined for the shores of France. We may imagine how enthusiastically the fine, handsome lad, heir, not only to the crown of England, but to that of the rich country they were bound to win, would be received by his noble, knightly, and yeomanly companions in arms. Nor can we doubt that the wild Irish and Welsh infantry would brandish their knives, and shout him a welcome. In number this force did not exceed thirty thousand. But we shall see what these could do against the chivalry and countless hosts of Philip of Valois.

Southampton was the place appointed for the embarkation of the English army, and thence the fleet sailed on the 24th of June, 1346. Edward left young Lionel, his third son, to take care of things at home, while he was away. This, of course, was a mere thing of state, Master Lionel being only eight years old; grave, bearded men, such as the lords Nevil and Percy, and several bishops, were in reality entrusted with the weighty cares of government. Nor did the war-loving king forget the prudent defence of his realm, by arms, as well as by wise heads; a sufficient military force being appointed for its protection during his absence.

The army which the king, his son, and some of the
greatest nobles and warriors of the time now commanded
for the conquest of France, was designed, as has been
said, to make its first attempt in the southern provinces.
Contrary winds, however, baffled that design, and on
the third day after their sailing from Southampton,
which they did merrily enough, drove them on their
own coast of Cornwall, instead of that of Gascony.
And here, after beating about for a while—nobody en-
joys coming back again, like a boomerang from its
mark—they were compelled to anchor, and suffer nearly
a weeks' detention.

On board the king's ship there was a French nobleman, named Sir Godfrey de Harcourt, who, having
given offence at his own court, had run away to that of
England, where he was received with great favour.
During the time they were detained by foul winds on
the Cornish coast, this Sir Godfrey set himself to alter.
Edward's plan as to the place of landing.   He advised
that the descent should be made upon Normandy; that
northern province being very rich and fertile, and
having the further advantage of being quite out of the
way of the rough skirmishers who had turned the
south upside down.   It was, therefore, quite unprepared for defence, its knighthood, with their retainers,
being drawn off to the field of action.   Its population,
too, were quiet and peaceable, occupied with the care of
their fields and flocks, and knowing nothing of sword,

lance, and cross-bow,—the cross-bow was that form of the weapon chiefly used on the Continent, and it was not considered so manly a one as the old English long-bow.

The advice was sound, and Edward had sense enough to take it. After having threatened the south, it was good policy on his part to swoop down upon the comparatively defenceless north. Winds and waves favoured him now, and speedily brought him and his fleet to La Hogue, in Normandy, on the 10th of July. If you look at the map you will see the little point jutting out, almost opposite to the Isle of Wight.

The king was the first to leap ashore. But "most haste" is not always "best speed." Not looking before he leaped, or making some other such simple blunder, down came his Highness (for it was not "Majesty" in those days) full length on the strand, with such force as to set the royal nose a-bleeding. That looked bad; and his superstitious nobles entreated him to return to his ship, and not think of effecting a landing after so unfortunate a beginning. Edward, however, was as superior to those about him in good sense as he was in military prowess, and he passed off his tumble with a jest, observing that the very ground itself was obviously longing for him.

The joke told; a good joke always will tell; and the disembarkation at once took place. The prince, who was aboard his father's ship, set foot, for the first time,

on the territory that he hoped would one day be his.
Nobles, knights, men-at-arms, and everybody else, including the wild Irish and Welsh, were duly got out
of the ships; and horses, armour, warlike stores, with
endless baggage, were all safely landed at last upon the
sandy beach, where they camped for that summer's
night. Rich tents were pitched for royalty and my
lords; while his cloak, and the glittering star-lit sky
overhead, were shelter enough for the humbler warrior
of that resolute little band.

A few days rest was allowed upon this spot; while,
to qualify them duly for the coming struggle, the
prince, and some other young nobles, had the honour of
knighthood conferred upon them by the king. Then
a council of war was held to decide on the course to
be pursued; and at this it was determined that the
Earl of Huntingdon, with about a hundred and twenty
men-at-arms, and four hundred archers, should remain
with the fleet, while the rest of the army moved on in
three divisions. One of these was under the command
of the king, with whom was his son, the new-made
knight, panting to do honour to his knighthood by
some signal feat of arms. Sir Godfrey de Harcourt
led the second; the Earl of Warwick the third. The
order of march was, for the king's division, or main
body, to move on in the centre; the Earl of Warwick's
division extended itself on the right; and that of Sir
Godfrey, which was a little in advance, acted upon the

left. The fleet followed their course along the coast, all uniting in one object,—that of plundering, burning, and destroying everything that came in their way.

They met with little opposition, for the simple country folks, who, as has been said, knew nothing of soldiers and battles, took to their heels and fled before the English ; the knights and men-at-arms who should have protected them from these cruel invaders being far away, fighting under the Duke of Normandy. So, between the fleet and the army,—spreading itself like a pestilence—the English took many rich towns, and acquired plunder to an enormous extent ; gold, silver, and valuable merchandise, which they carefully packed up, sent on board their attendant ships, and rejoicingly conveyed to England. Spoil was so abundant that the very camp followers "turned up their noses " at rich furred gowns, which, in those days, were worn ; and there was no lack of provision for this locust-like swarm either, seeing that those who fled could not take their well-stored houses and barns with them.

King Philip meanwhile was not idle. When news was brought him that the English had landed in Normandy, and were destroying that province at their pleasure, he summoned every earl, baron, and knight, who owed him service, to march with him against them. The lords eagerly obeyed his command, but some were so distant from the scene of action that they could not attend the king in time to check the advance of the enemy, who soon made their way to within a few miles of Paris. The citizens were terribly frightened when they found the English at their very gates ; the more so that Philip was just setting out to St. Denis, about four miles off, to join the lords who were assembled there. Expecting to be swallowed at a mouthful by those terrible islanders,—upon their knees the poor citizens besought the king to stay and take care of them, for if he did not, the English would certainly come upon them, and make themselves masters of his fine city of Paris.

King Philip thought he should best protect his fine city of Paris and its trembling inhabitants by joining his army at St. Denis, and fighting the invaders. He told the suppliants so ; and to cheer their hearts, declared that the English would never touch them, nor their city either. This turned out quite true, as Edward, having burned some villages near its walls, passed on northwards, by Beauvais, where he hung twenty of his own people for having set fire to the abbey of St. Messien, contrary to his express commands that no church or monastery should be injured. Beauvais was attacked, but its inhabitants, with a good military bishop at their head, showed fight so gallantly that the English were beaten back. The people of Poix, a little further on, either not being in a mood for fighting, or not prepared for it, thought best to buy off the enemy

EDWARD III. BESTOWING KNIGHTHOOD ON THE BLACK PRINCE.

A certain sum was agreed upon, on the faith of which the town and its two fortresses were to be left untouched. The king and the young prince slept there quietly that night, and next morning withdrew the army to pursue its march.   No sooner, however, were they out of the way than those excellent people of Poix recovered from their fright, and plainly told the few English who had been left behind to receive the ransom, that they would not pay one penny of what they had promised ; and so saying, they fell fiercely upon the little troop. This was shabby.   Fortunately for the English, who defended themselves gallantly, their rear-guard was not far off, and they hastily sent to it for succour.   Lord Reginald Cobham, and Sir Thomas Holland who commanded, hastened to the help of their comrades, with loud shouts of "Treason, treason !" and speedily punished the townsmen's bad faith by slaying great numbers of them, burning their town, and pulling down their castles to the very ground.

This was severe ; but faith ought to be kept, even with an enemy.   Those who break their word must not complain if they suffer for it.

One of these castles, when the army first took possession, was found to be garrisoned by two young ladies, the beautiful daughters of its absent lord.   They were chivalrously protected from the rude soldiery by that glorious John Chandos, of whom we shall hear again ; and the Lord Basset, who brought them to the

king's presence. Edward received the ladies with all
courtesy, asking them whither they would go, and
commanded that they should be safely conducted to
their chosen place of refuge.

Edward's career, in the north-west of France, had so
far been highly successful. Still, in the neighbourhood
of Paris, it was materially checked by the French
having broken down the bridges over the numerous
rivers that intersect that part of the country, and from
which the district received its former name, of the *Isle*
of France. At Poissy, about twenty miles from the
capital, the English almost stuck fast; but the army
was extricated by a feint on the part of its leader.
Edward made as though he were going off in the opposite direction, then returned hastily, patched up the
bridge, and got, for that time, out of the way of Philip
and his avenging host. But though he escaped here,
he soon found that the net was being drawn closer
around him. Broken bridges stopped him on every
hand, while those hundred-thousand angry Frenchmen
were almost upon his heels. It seemed the turn of the
English to be swallowed up now, for they were finally
placed between the bridgeless Somme and the French
army, eager to avenge, upon the king of England and
the beardless boy his son, the injuries inflicted by
them upon the French nation.

Many English heads had been laid low, spite of the
triumphant character of their inroad, so that the origi-

nal odds of thirty thousand against one hundred thousand, were fearfully increased at this juncture. Fighting or starving seemed the only alternatives offered to the English, and they were not inclined to accept either. In this dilemma Sir Godfrey de Harcourt and the Earl of Warwick, with a couple of thousand men-at-arms and archers, were sent down stream to see whether bridge or ford, of some kind or other, could not be discovered. The search was fruitless; and when, on their return to the army, they had communicated the result of it, the king, who was full of thought and care, ordered immediate preparations to be made for decamping, as King Philip was already within six miles of them. There really seemed to be nothing now but a run for it.

Those iron-clad and iron-hearted men of the fourteenth century *prayed* as well as fought. Before the sun had risen upon the dispirited little army, there was heard not only the trumpet-sound for breaking up the camp, but the quiet voice of the priest imploring mercy from the God of heaven, and blessing the kneeling worshippers. What a heart-felt "Good Lord, deliver us!" would ascend from that imperilled band! and who shall say that those prayers were not heard?

In stern military order the march commenced: men-at-arms, archers, and their shaggy comrades with the big knives, streamed out of Airaines; and even the hindermost files, those whom loitering or business had thrown into the veriest rear, had cleared it for a good two hours, before the French vanguard, in equal military order, entered the town. The enemy had escaped them, that was plain. So, instead of exchanging blows with the English, their only revenge was to sit down and eat up the good things that were, of necessity, left behind. There were barrels of wine; joints on the spit, just ready for roasting; bread and pastry half-baked in the ovens; and tables, vainly spread for the nobles and knights now careering away in the distance; compelled to fly, and yet not so disheartened as to be incapable of attacking a little town that stood in their way, knocking it all to shivers, and then taking up their lodging in it for the night.

King Philip fixed his quarters at Airaines, and, doubtless, the excellent cheer thus provided for them by the retreating foe, was (without any fear of the usual consequence of things going down the "wrong throat") heartily enjoyed by his followers. We cannot for a moment suppose that his Highness of France would condescend to eat any of these English "leavings!"

At Oisemont, a town between Airaines and Abbeville, King Edward afresh held a council, and ordered the prisoners, whom his troops in their skirmishing about the country had seized, to be brought before him, that he might question them as to the possibility of getting over the river. He asked these, very courteously, if they knew of any ford below Abbeville where he and

his army might cross the Somme, adding, that to him
who would conduct him to such a place he would give
his liberty, and that of any twenty, whomsoever he
might choose, of his companions.

Liberty is sweet; and, thereupon, up spoke a common
fellow (named Gobin Agace) to this effect :—

"Sir,—I promise you, under peril of my life, to
guide you to a place where you and your whole army
may pass the river without hurt. There are certain
fords where twelve men a-breast may cross twice in the
day, and not have water above their knees; but when
the tide is in, the river is so full and deep that no one
can cross it. When the tide is out, the river is so low
that it may be passed on horseback, or on foot without danger. The bottom of this ford is very hard, of
gravel and white stones, over which all your carriages
may safely pass, and from thence it is called Blanchtaque. You must, therefore, set out early, so as to be
at the ford before sunrise."

Overjoyed at such good news, the king readily promised the speaker a round sum of money, in addition
to his liberty, provided his statement, as to this admirable ford, proved correct.

Gobin, as it happened, was a true man—to his own
interest! We must say nothing of his king and country. Some people would sell the whole world, if they
only saved their own precious necks thereby. This was
precisely Gobin's condition.

After two or three hours of anxious, uneasy rest, king, prince, knights, and meaner men alike, arose. Midnight though it was, the trumpets were heard sounding loudly for the march; and by break of day all were moving on, under the leadership of the illustrious Gobin, to the ford of Blanchtaque. The brightening sunbeams of an early August morning played upon the broad waters of the river; for, alas! the Somme was a tidal stream, and, by the time the faithful Gobin had brought up his royal and military train, the tide was at its height. To make bad worse, at the other side of the swelling flood appeared Sir Godemar du Fay, a great Norman baron, to whose especial care it had been committed to baffle the King of England at this point. Sir Godemar was at the head of a large force of men-at-arms and infantry, backed by the burly, well-armed townsmen of Abbeville, and a zealous swarm of country-folks in their smock-frocks. What sort of weapons was wielded by these good fellows in the smock-frocks, historians do not tell us. Most likely they snatched up their pitchforks and goads; which, rude enough considered as instruments of war, were yet capable, when poised by such brawny arms, of inflicting very ugly wounds on any of the enemy unfortunate enough to come within their range. The pass leading from the ford was well manned by a posse of Genoese cross-bowmen.

The brimming river, and the armed host upon its

opposite bank, formed a rather disheartening prospect. But it was a case of "nothing venture, nothing win;" though an experienced commander, such as the still young monarch of England, was not going to do anything rashly. The river had to be crossed, and those threatening Frenchmen on the other side had—in school-boy phrase—to be "thrashed" before his brave followers were free from peril. The tide at length turned, as the highest tide will do; and, eagerly watching its slow retreating course, the keen eye of our Edward at once marked out the precise time when he must dash forward and dare everything. A footing in the stream became possible, and then, in the name of "God and St. George," the horsemen, king, prince, and all, leaped into the shallowing water. And on the opposite bank, making the air ring with shouts of "God and St. Denis," in sprang the French men-at-arms; quite as ready (observes an old writer) for a tilting match in the water, as on dry land. Fierce blows and thrusts were exchanged, as they *plowtered* in the stream; and the sword of the young prince, it is said, was then first stained with blood.

It must, from that time have assumed a very different aspect in his eyes. Before, it was the mere glittering plaything of a boy; henceforth, it was the terrible death-dealing weapon of a man!

The forcing of this passage over the Somme was no easy matter. French, against English valour was, that

day, well matched. The English archers, however, at
last turned the day in favour of their countrymen.
Their fearful storm of arrows compelled even the
bravest of the French knights to give way; and the
English fairly won the opposite bank, driving their
opponents before them in all directions. In the hot
pursuit which followed, terrible slaughter was done
upon the flying enemy. Knights, men-at-arms, fat
burghers from Abbeville, and simple peasants fresh
from their flocks and fields, found, that day, one common doom, from sharp English lances and swift-winged
English arrows.

The river was crossed. But it was only just in time,
seeing that some of the hindmost were set upon, and
slain by, the light cavalry of the advancing French
army.

King Philip was not particularly pleased when he
found that his prey had escaped him. Nor did it add
to his satisfaction, on his own arrival at the river's
bank, to perceive that the tide was already flowing
back again, so as to leave him no chance, save that of
going round to the bridge at Abbeville. In his first
paroxysm of rage he bethought him of hanging Sir
Godemar Fay, for not having better disputed the passage committed to his keeping; but the intercession of
his brother knights saved that nobleman from so disgraceful a fate.

Honest Gobin—well, he was honest to his new

master, though a little treacherous to his old one—
duly received the promised reward, and a good horse
into the bargain. His service was worth paying for
handsomely. Then solemn thanks were returned by
the English to God who had delivered them from so
pressing a danger. With that baffled French host, on
the other side of the now flowing tide, the English
must have felt somewhat as did the Israelites when
the returning waves of the Red Sea, over which they
had passed dry-shod, rolled in again upon "Pharaoh and
his horsemen," swallowing them up in its triumphant
waters.

The deliverance of the English however, great and
thankworthy as it was, was yet but a temporary one.
Philip, speeding away over the round-about bridge at
Abbeville, was soon heard of again in their rear; and
then a stand, to meet him, and fight for it, was made,
near Crecy in Ponthieu. For "now," said Edward,
" I am on my mother's lawful inheritance, given as her
marriage-portion, and I am resolved to defend it against
Philip of Valois."

The Battle of Crecy.

THE celebrated battle-field of Creçy lies about eight miles north of Abbeville. Edward's army here drawn up, was much smaller than that of the enemy. As has been said, it is probable that it fell considerably short of its original thirty thousand; while the French—if rumour did not exaggerate their numbers—amounted to a hundred and twenty thousand. As things turned out, we might afford to make them a present of the odd twenty. thousand; and believe that it was only one hundred thousand gallant Frenchmen and their allies that our mere handful destroyed on that memorable day.

The comparative insignificance of the English, however, made it all the more important that they should be posted as advantageously as possible; the Earl of Warwick and Sir Godfrey de Harcourt, therefore, rode over the ground, noticing, with keen practised eyes, how every yard of it might be turned to the best account. That business settled, they were in pretty good

ENGLISH ARMY CROSSING THE SOMME.

Page 51

heart about the matter. Provisions were plentiful in the country; and even had they not been, their own stores were far from being exhausted. So, having first ascertained that Philip had no intention of giving battle immediately, they pitched their tents that night in the plain.

There, all was soon eager preparation for the anticipated struggle of the next day. Arms were examined. A faulty lance-shaft might have brought destruction upon the knight who wielded it, a weather-rotted bowstring would have rendered one arrow useless; and with their inferior numbers, not one lance, nor one greygoose-winged arrow could they afford to throw away. Then there was a great clattering and overhauling of armour. Cuirasses, cuisses,—the pieces that protected the legs—helmets or gauntlets, wanting a strap here, or a buckle there, had to be made " right and tight," and polished up into the bargain. These were the personal cares of squires, and men-at-arms ; the squires waiting upon the knights their masters, the men-atarms waiting upon themselves. The king and prince were occupied in giving a great supper to the leaders of their brave troops, and at that entertainment no fears of to-morrow's clash of arms spoiled their knightly appetites. They ate well, they drank well, and then retired from the royal presence to tent or cloak, as each one best pleased, with the determination of fighting well next morning.

The cares and hospitalities of the day ended, the king, in his solitude, first kneeled down in devout prayer to God, that He would give him victory in the forthcoming battle, and then, like the rest, threw himself upon his bed about midnight.

Early next morning, August 26th, he and the prince joined in prayers, and received the Holy Communion. The greater part of his army did the same; and then the trumpets sounded to arms, and for each division of the army to take the ground marked out for it.

There were three of these divisions. The first was commanded by the Prince of Wales; and under him were some noble and knightly warriors, whose descendants—if there be any of the old blood still remaining—may well be proud of their ancestors at Crecy. There were the Earls of Warwick and Oxford, Sir Godfrey de Harcourt, the Lords-Reginald Cobham, Thomas Holland, Stafford, Mauley, Delawarre, Bartholomew, Burghersh, Robert Neville, Thomas Clifton, Bourchier, Latimer, Sir John Chandos, and other knights notable in their day, but whose very names are now extinguished. The brave boy was bravely supported. This division numbered about eight hundred men-at-arms, two thousand archers, and one thousand Welshmen. All at once moved on in good order, to their appointed post; each lord displaying his banner and pennon,—the pennon was a forked streamer attached to the upper part of the lance,—and marching in the centre of his men.

The second division was commanded by the Earls of Southampton, and Arundel; the Lords Roos, Willoughby, Basset, St. Albans, Lascels, Multon, Sir Lewis Tufton, and many others. It comprised eight hundred men-at-arms, and twelve hundred archers.

The king himself headed the reserve, or third division, of about seven hundred men-at-arms, and two thousand archers. The men-at-arms (as was sometimes the custom, like that of our old-fashioned dragoons), were dismounted, and prepared to fight on foot. The baggage of the entire army, with the waggons and horses, was placed in the rear within an enclosure, to which there was but one entrance, and *that*, we may believe, was well guarded. Trenches were hastily dug on both sides as an additional protection to the little army; and in front were placed a few cannon, then a novel invention, used, perhaps for the first time, during Edward's previous wars in Scotland.

His forces being thus marshalled in battle-array, the king, wearing neither helmet nor coat of mail, but simply his usual hood and dress, mounted his riding-horse, or *hackney* as it was called; the magnificent charger being reserved for the battle-field; and passing at a foot's pace through their ranks, with his marshals on either hand, addressed his men, encouraging them to guard the honour of their sovereign, and defend his right to the throne of France. His cheerful looks, and still more cheering words, went straight to the hearts

of his stalwart fellows, who drew fresh courage from
his animating appeals. For, if truth must be told,
some of them were becoming a little down-hearted;
the numbers against them being so terribly overpowering as somewhat to damp the confidence inspired by
previous successes.

As by this time it was near ten o'clock (the usual
dinner-hour of that period), the king ended by bidding
his men eat and drink heartily; and then he retired to
his own post. Advice so agreeable was instantly acted
upon; and after they had eaten and drunken to their
heart's content, they packed up their pots, barrels,
dishes, platters, and such things in the waggons, and
then sat down on the ground with their helmets and
arms beside them, that they might be the fresher when
the enemy came up. And so they prepared to meet
the formidable Philip of Valois.

That same Saturday morning the King of France
also rose betimes; and as soon as he and his army had
had prayers, they moved on towards the English. When
within four miles of Abbeville, they too were formed
in order of battle, and then continued their march; the
infantry in front, to keep out of the way of their own
cavalry. Four knights whom Philip had sent forward
to reconnoitre, now returned, bringing him word that
they had caught sight of the English, drawn up as we
have described them, on the sloping ground near
Crecy; and they advised him to halt his troops for the

night, where they were, for if they went on, they would
certainly be too tired to attack the English with any
advantage. Upon this, the order was given to "halt
banner, in the name of God and St. Denis." St.
Denis was the patron saint of the French, as St.
George was of the English. Those in front halted
accordingly. But they who were in the rear, vowed
they would not halt, till they were as forward as the
front. And with that they kept pushing on.

Oh, what mischief came of this piece of stupidity!
By the pressure from behind, spite of the efforts of the
king and his generals to stop them, the front ranks
were driven on until, in utter disorder, they came within sight of the enemy. The appearance of Edward's
well-ordered battalions rather checked their ardour;
and they fell back, in a confused manner, upon the
rear, to whom they communicated their own panic;
panics being eminently catching. Some few did what
all might have done had they chosen, and made their
way to the front; but the greater part hung back.
There was unaccountable confusion and disorder
throughout the whole French army; so that their vast
numbers did them more harm than good. An attempt
was made to rally them; and at last, on they went,
but in a sad pell-mell sort of fashion, hither and
thither, as each lord, baron, or knight thought fit.

Seeing them advance, the English rose from the
ground where they were sitting, and fell into their

ranks. All was calmness and order here; and the
boy-prince, whose division was to bear the first brunt
of battle, took the post that had been assigned to him.
His archers were in the van, his men-at-arms in the
rear. The Earls of Northampton and Arundel, were
stationed so as to support the prince, in case of need.
The king formed his division on a height at a little
distance, where he could overlook the field, and bring
up his reserve, or not, as the battle might turn. He
himself stood by a windmill, which, not long ago, was
said to be still remaining on this memorable spot.

The attack was made by the French about three
o'clock in the afternoon. Their first line consisted of
fifteen thousand Genoese cross-bowmen; and these the
king bade his marshals order forward, "in the name
of God and St. Denis," to begin the battle. The
Genoese, however, were in no condition for doing so.
They had had a long day's march on foot, heavily
armed; and were so worn out with fatigue, that they
plainly told the constable they were not fit for anything. The Earl of Alençon, who commanded the
second division, hearing this, exclaimed in a pet,—
"This is what one gets by employing such scoundrels,
who fail us when most wanted." And, among them,
they managed to drive the poor, tired, drenched
Genoese (for there was a heavy thunder-storm at the
time) on towards the English. The storm, which added
to their confusion, soon, however, cleared off, and the

PREPARATIONS ON THE EVE OF BATTLE.

sun shone out bright, but full in the faces of the French, so dazzling and blinding them, that it was even worse than the rain.

At length, spurred on by their commanders, the Genoese prepared for action, and sprang with a shout towards the English, who stood firm, never minding their noise. Again they leaped forward with a great cry as before; but the English, with that boy at their head, stirred not a foot. It was plain there was no frightening them with mere noise. A third time there was a bound and a cry, and then—not noise alone—thousands of bolts from their cross-bows, fell upon the enemy. Now was the time for the boy to prove himself a man. The word of command was given; and, advancing one step, the English archers poured in, among the foe, such a shower of arrows that, as an old writer says, it was like a snow-storm : keen, stinging arrows, for soft snow-flakes. The Genoese could not stand this. Heads, arms, legs, broad chests, pierced by the long, sharp shafts,—they fled in dismay ; cutting their bow-strings, already weakened by the rain, and throwing down their useless weapons, as they turned their ignominious backs upon the English yeomen.

Philip, in a rage at their flight, called out to his mounted men-at-arms to "kill those rascals." And, nothing loth, the horsemen rode in among their wearied, discomfited comrades, cutting them down without

mercy; while still, amid the mingled mass of men
and horses, hot and thick fell the merciless English
arrows; hottest and thickest wherever the press was
greatest.   Into that wounded, writhing heap, too,
plunged sullenly the clumsy stone balls of those new,
and alarming great guns in front; whose noise, to un-
accustomed ears was, we are told, as "though God
thundered!"   Down went men and horses among the
baffled Genoese, one overthrowing another; and he
who was once down, had no chance of rising again.
Then, when the rout and disorder was at its height,
was the time for the Irish and Welshmen.   Passing
through the ranks of their own men-at-arms and
archers, their great knives, if not very military weapons, proved fatal, to many a gaily accoutred prostrate
horseman.   No distinction of rank was there.   Noble
and squire alike were remorselessly slain by these
rough soldiers, whose zeal was anything but pleasing.
to their own knightly sovereign.   King Edward could
not abide such wholesale slaughter.   Possibly (for
meaner motives will sometimes mingle with generous
ones), he regretted the loss of the abundant ransom,
which such prisoners as those who had perished under
the cruel knives of his half-savage infantry, would have
furnished.   For, according to the custom of the times,
knights and gentlemen, when taken prisoners, were
allowed to purchase their freedom by sums of money
proportioned to their rank and wealth.

It was here that the brave, blind old king of Bohemia, who marched under Philip's banner, met his fate.   Unable, through blindness, to make his own way into the fight, he bade two faithful knights lead him on, that he might strike at least one good sword-stroke at the enemy.   They placed him between them, fastened their horse bridles to his, that they might not be separated in the throng, and then, in all three- dashed, fought valiantly, and all fell on the battle-field, where next morning their bodies were found on one spot; their three horses still linked together, standing quietly by them.   The Lord Charles of Bohemia, son to the king, was bringing up a force to aid the French; but perceiving, when at a little distance that the battle was going against them, he discreetly turned aside and went his way.

The young prince meanwhile was so hard pressed by the French second line, under the Earl of Alençon, which had advanced to back the flying rabble of Genoese, that the Earls of Arundel and Northampton moved up their division to support him.   The battle was terribly hot here, and the king of France himself, hovering on their skirts, was eagerly looking for an opening to lead his third division in among them.   The English archers, however, formed an impenetrable wall against him, that he vainly endeavoured to break through; and the struggle lay chiefly between the prince's force and that under Alençon.   The young fellow was sorely put to it; and fearing for so precious a life, the Earl of Warwick sent off a knight, post haste to the king, entreating him to bring up the reserve, to rescue his son from so imminent a danger.

"Is my son dead, or wounded, or unhorsed?" was the king's answer to this urgent request.

"No," replied the knight, "but he is so hardly matched that he cannot long hold out without you."

"Sir Thomas," was the rejoinder, "go back to your comrades, and tell them they must not send to me for help so long as my son is alive. He must this day win his spurs, and I am determined, if God will, that the glory of this day shall be his own, and that of those who are with him."

The knight galloped back again with his message, which seemed to put fresh life into the princely lad and his brave companions. Fiercer blows were dealt, hotter and more strenuous was the attack, till, ere long, the unruly multitude of French knights, and squires, and men, began to give way before them. The Earls of Flanders and Alençon, who had turned the flank of the prince's archers, were slain, together with many of their best knights; and the entire first and second French lines were forced back. Philip made a vigorous effort to turn the fortunes of the day; but it was of no use; the whole French army was utterly routed and driven off the field in confusion. The royal standard narrowly escaped capture. Its bearer was struck down

in the fight, but while French and English eagerly contended for so glorious a prize, the one to seize, the
other to rescue it, a French knight hastily with his
sword, cut the banner from its shaft, wrapped it round
his body, and rode off with it. King Philip himself
was wounded, his horse was killed under him by an
arrow, and as he sprang on another, Sir John de Hainault snatched at the reins, and forced him off, telling
him by way of comfort, that if he had lost one battle,
he might gain another. And away they both swept to
Amiens, with a retinue of only sixty knights and men-
at-arms, in place of the splendid array of the morning.

It was a murderous and cruel battle; for the
desperate English gave no quarter, nor would they
ransom any. At night-fall, as the noise died away,
they looked upon the field as their own, and lighted up
torches and great fires, intending to bivouac where they
stood; for in their circumstances they dared not venture
on immediate pursuit. The king, who had never even
put on his helmet, then descended from his post of
observation, and leading forward his battalion, which
like himself, had looked on only, throughout that hard-
fought day, advanced to meet his son. He folded him
in his arms, and kissed him lovingly, saying, in the
quaint language of those times, "Sweet son, God give
you good perseverance! You are indeed my own son,
for very valiantly have you this day acquitted yourself.
You are worthy to be a king!"

Such words, from such a father, fell pleasantly upon the ear of the panting, battle-stained boy. Most modestly was the loving commendation received, and then he fell upon his knees, to beg his father's blessing. That, we may be sure, was heartily given.

The rejoicings of the English on this eventful night were orderly rejoicings, for the king had utterly forbidden all noise or riot. And they were fittingly mingled with many thanksgivings to God, who had given them so wonderful a victory. Their losses were trivial. Those of the French were immense. Clumsy stone cannon balls, lance, sword, sheaves of unerring arrows, and even those big knives, had done their work upon kings, princes, nobles, knights, and common men, to the number of forty thousand. There, as the old poet has sung,—

> · Sceptre and crown
> Had tumbled down,
> And in the dust were equal laid,
> With the poor crooked scythe and spade! "

The next morning which was Sunday, proved so foggy that none could see twenty yards before him, and this circumstance threw another considerable body of French into the hands of the English. Edward had ordered out a strong detachment of five hundred lances, and two thousand archers, under his two marshals, who were directed to scour the neighbourhood, lest any of the enemy should be collecting again to make a fresh stand against him. French troops, ignorant of the total overthrow of their army, had that morning left Abbeville and St. Riguier to join Philip at Creçy; and these in the mist, taking the English for their own friends, were almost among them before they discovered their fatal mistake. The encounter between the two was short, but sharp, and ended in the slaughter of great numbers of the French, not one of whom would have escaped, had not the fog (which had betrayed them to their discomfiture) favoured the flight of a few, who thus saved themselves. A second, well-appointed party of French, under the Archbishop of Rouen, and the Grand Prior of France, met with the same fate from the marshals' detachment, who cut them almost all to pieces, including their right reverend leader. Others, found wandering in the fields, where they had lain all night, were also savagely put to the sword. In short, it is said that more were slain on that Sunday morning, than had fallen in the battle itself.

The returning marshals informed the king, who was just coming from prayers, of their successful and sanguinary proceedings. And then, as there was no fear of a second army to be encountered, by his command, heralds, attended by their secretaries, slowly traversed the field to take account of the dead. The name and rank of the slain knights could only be ascertained by their coats of arms, emblazoned upon the shield, or surcoat; and when this sad task was ended, by Edward's

order, the chiefest of them were reverently laid to rest
in consecrated ground attached to the monastery of
Montenay, close at hand. The king himself, with his
great lords, all clad in black, took part in the solemn
ceremony, by way of doing honour to his brave, though
unfortunate enemies. Three days' truce was granted
for burying the dead. It is said to be from this time
that the Prince of Wales, who, young as he was, had
shown himself so terrible at Creçy, was known among
the French by the title—now so familiar to our ears
—of the Black Prince.

Hot from their fierce, but brilliant encounter at Creçy,
Edward, on the following Monday, August 28th,
marched his brave Britons straight to the siege of
Calais. It was a four days' march, and they did a little
burning and plundering by the way.

V.

The Siege of Calais.

HE governor of Calais was a brave Burgundian knight, named Sir John de Vienne; and other valiant knights with squires to match, but whose names are scarcely worth preserving, served under him. The town was strongly fortified, and these grim men in iron cases, were determined to hold it against the King of England, and his victorious son.

That king, however, and that son had equally determined to take it; and therefore—in military phrase—"sat down" (which means something like, standing up!) before Calais, on the 1st of August, 1346. They did this with all calmness and order, as though they could afford to take their time about it. The camp was marked out, tents were pitched; and even a sort of town composed of huts, thatched with straw, or broom, soon sprang up under those marvellous English hands, impertinently close to the walls of the besieged city. Markets were established here for all comers; and in them, fish, flesh, fowl, bread, clothing—all sorts of things, either from the surrounding country, or from over seas, might be had for *money*. As for those who had no money, it is to be presumed that they would have been as ill off in the king's market before Calais, as in any other. From this comfortable kind of settlement the English made frequent sorties (that is another military phrase, and literally means—going out), doing much mischief in the neighbourhood, and picking up spoil for themselves; occasionally, it must be owned, though not often, getting the worst of it. They made no attempt to storm the town. They had neither men, nor engines of war enough for that. Their grand object was to compel the surrender of the garrison by cutting off their supply of provisions. This is called, blockading a place. If he failed to starve the defenders of Calais into submission, Edward hoped that at any rate their sufferings would draw the King of France thither to attempt their relief, and that would afford him another opportunity of beating Philip.

The blockade was strict, and so experienced a commander as John de Vienne, at once saw that he must make diligent preparation to baffle the well-laid plans of the two Edwards. If provisions could not be brought into the town, it was plain that they must make what they had go as far as possible, by reducing the number of consumers. The less meat, the fewer mouths; that was how the difficulty must be met. Of course, soldiers who could fight, were to be retained at any cost; and the rich inhabitants whose wealth had enabled them to lay in store of eatables and drinkables, or to purchase the good things that were occasionally at great risk smuggled in, spite of the English, were at liberty to stay if they liked. As for those who could neither fight, nor contribute to the general stock, they must troop, and the sooner they were got rid of, the better.

Prompt execution followed resolution. It was a hard thing, but military necessity is harder still; so one Wednesday morning, seventeen hundred of those who were of no use in the defence—who had only craving mouths, instead of the soldiers, trained right hand, or the merchant's money bags,—were driven out of the town, weeping and wailing, to await the mercy of the English camp, through which they must pass. Poor men, women and children,—it was a strange sight, that stream of miserable, forlorn, human beings, from grey-heads to infants, unconscious of their troubles, in their mother's arms; and the staring English, in utter astonishment, asked what in the world they meant by thus coming right into the midst of the enemy; why had they left the town?

The answer was simple enough : "Because they had nothing to eat." The English were enemies, bent, spite of all the Frenchmen that Philip of Valois could scrape together, on taking his strong town of Calais. But they were also *men;* and their good, honest hearts, were touched by the distress of these unhappy people, mercilessly turned out by their countrymen to perish. To permit them to pass on, unharmed, to a place of refuge, was much; but it was not all. That noble King Edward, in addition to this, ordered the poor wretches a hearty dinner; and then, when the hungry "enemy" had been "fed," (we know Who has bidden us do that!) he gave to each of them two pence—worth more than as many shillings in these days—to carry them on their doleful journey. That man deserved to take Calais. No wonder that many fervent prayers were offered up by these unfortunate French men and women for their benefactor; English invader and claimant of their Philip's crown though he was. It was indeed a good work that Edward did that Wednesday. "Blessed is he that considereth the poor and needy." To such, a recompense is surely promised.

The character of this great king and that of his great son, warlike as they both were, was one of general humanity; and this beneficence to the poor, helpless wretches driven out of Calais, was an illustrious example of it. War is a cruel trade; but there are two ways of carrying it on: Like *men* and like wild beasts.

The siege of Calais was protracted. Blockading is slow work; and as more men, more money, more everything was wanted, the young prince was despatched to England to seek fresh succours. These, thanks to the liberality of parliament, were abundantly obtained;

FRENCH KNIGHT RESCUING KING PHILIP'S STANDARD.

Page 69

for Englishmen, to their very heart's core, enjoyed the successful contest with France, and did not much care what they paid for it.

During the course of this tedious eleven months' siege, an incident occurred which is worth recording, as an interesting exhibition of the knightly manners of the time.

It has been named that the Duke of Normandy, eldest son of the French king, was engaged at the other end of the country laying siege to Aiguillon, a town in Edward's French possessions, where all the fighting had been going on, until Godfrey de Harcourt suggested Normandy. From this place the duke was recalled by Philip, who required all the forces he could gather to resist that formidable father, and no less formidable son, who had been carrying everything before them in the north. The siege was accordingly *raised*, as it is termed—that is, given up; and the celebrated Sir Walter Manny, who commanded in the town, making a dash after the retreating French, took a handful of good prisoners, whom his people brought back with them to the castle. Among these prisoners was a Norman knight, a very important personage indeed ; and as Sir Walter longed to be with his countrymen before Calais, he cleverly contrived to join them by means of this same prisoner, whom he courteously bade fix his own ransom. The sum named by the knight was a large one. Great men did not like to be let off too cheaply on these occasions, because *that* looked as if they were worth little. And in reply, Sir Walter told him, that if he would procure permission for his captor and twenty others to ride straight through France to Calais, without stopping by the way or conducting themselves otherwise than as ordinary travellers, he would let him go without any ransom at all, and thank him into the bargain. If the knight failed to procure this safe-conduct, he was to return to his prison within one month.

The terms were tempting. Off set the Norman knight after his duke, got the required passport, and posted back again with it to Sir Walter, who gave him his freedom as he had promised.

Sir Walter then with twenty horsemen took the road to Calais. He went to work frankly; told every one who he was; and wherever he stopped for the night, on showing his safe-conduct, was allowed to proceed next morning. On arriving at Orleans, however, there was a change. No respect was in that city shown to the duke's permission for him to pass free; nay, he was even arrested and sent immediately to Paris, where he was thrown into prison.

The Duke of Normandy, of course, heard of the contempt with which his safe-conduct had been treated, and of the usage to which so renowned a knight had been subjected. He was terribly put out by it. It was contrary to all the laws of knighthood, and he hastened to the king his father, urgently pleading for the liberation of the prisoner, otherwise, as he said, people would think he had granted the safe-conduct solely for the purpose of betraying Sir Walter.

The king's answer to his son was not very consolatory. He simply replied that he intended putting Sir Walter Manny to death, as he considered him one of the most important of his enemies.

The indignant duke's rejoinder was, that if any harm was done to the knight, neither he nor any of his people should ever again bear arms against the king of England. And with that, father and son quarrelled violently—the duke at last flinging out with a renewed declaration that he would not serve in the king's armies so long as Sir Walter Manny was kept in prison.

Things remained in this state for some time; but at length the king became ashamed of his discourteous behaviour, allowed Sir Walter to go free, and reimbursed him the expenses to which his shameful imprisonment had put him. He went further, and, by way of plastering the wound which he had himself inflicted, even invited Sir Walter to the royal dinner-table, pressing upon him rich gifts and jewels, which the knight accepted, subject to the pleasure of his own sovereign; for he did not know whether Edward would like him to keep them. Edward did not choose that a knight of his should receive presents from the enemy. So, right royally saying to him, " Sir Walter, we have

enough, thank God, both for you and for ourselves,"
he bade him return them to their donor; intimating
to Sir Walter, that the faithful servants of the King of
England must look to their own master, not to the
King of France, for their reward. Sir Walter accordingly sent back the jewels by a cousin of his, who was
only too glad to keep them himself, when Philip bade
him do so.

The siege of Calais still held on its slow course,
according to the manner of sieges; its monotony being
varied, towards the close of the year, by the arrival in
camp of Queen Philippa and her son the prince.
Philippa had had her hands full during the absence of
her lord—the hard battle of Neville's Cross, in Dur-
ham, in which the King of Scotland was taken prisoner,
having been fought under her own eyes. Her reception in the camp was one befitting both her rank and
the heroic courage she had recently displayed; and as
she brought in her train many great ladies of the
court, there were brave doings, in the way of feast
and tournament, to celebrate so agreeable a visit.

The King of France was not disposed to give up
Calais quietly, but his attempts to relieve it proved
fruitless. He raised an immense army, far outnum-
bering that of the enemy, for this purpose; but the
English were so skilfully intrenched by their great
leader, that Philip could not get near the town. It
was in vain that he invited Edward to " come out and

fight;" Edward knew better, and told him so, than
to sacrifice the advantages which had cost him so much
time and treasure. So this vast French army, after the
citizens had admired its numerous banners fluttering
in the moonlight, decamped, leaving the people of
Calais, who sorrowingly watched its departure, to do
the best they could for themselves.

Bad was the best, for the blockade had been so strict
that their provisions were well-nigh expended. Yea,
horses, dogs, cats, and viler creatures, had been already
eaten by the wretched inhabitants, who could no longer
endure starvation. So they entreated John de Vienne,
their governor, to mount the walls and make signs that
he wished a parley with the besiegers. That word
parley is a French word, bodily imported into our
English, with the slight alteration of our spelling it with
a *y*, instead of a *z*, and really means, talk! So Sir
John reluctantly did as they would have him; for he
was a brave knight, and would rather have held out
the town to the last.

The governor's summons was answered by Sir Walter Manny and Lord Basset, to whom he spoke man-
fully, saying that the king his master had entrusted
the defence of Calais to him and his companions,
and they had done their duty till they were now
near famishing with hunger; and he prayed that
the King of England would be content with possession of the castle and town, in which he would find

great store of riches, letting the garrison depart unmolested.

Sir Walter had no very agreeable answer to this entreaty. He assured John de Vienne that the King of England his master was so enraged at the loss of men, time, and money, which this siege of Calais had cost him, that he would offer the garrison no terms save those of unconditional surrender; for him to put to death whom he pleased, and admit to ransom whom he pleased.

The spirit of the governor was roused by this cruel declaration, and he told Sir Walter that he and his companions had only done what English knights and squires in similar circumstances would have done— held out as long as there was a stick or stone standing, and a mouthful of food for any one. But still, famishing as they were, they would endure much more, rather than that the meanest horse-boy in the place should fare worse than they. And he besought Sir Walter to represent their hard case to the King of England, of whose knighthood he had so high an opinion, that he could not believe he would deal so harshly with them as he had threatened.

The king, however, was really as angry as man could be, and he told Sir Walter that the garrison of Calais must take his first terms or none. Sir Walter expostulated with him, that if he dealt such hard measures to his conquered enemies, his own knights would rather unwillingly go out on dangerous service, expecting, if taken by the French, to be put to death, just as he, if he did not relent, put to death the brave fellows who had so long held Calais against him. It would certainly be death for death, if the fortunes of war turned against them.

Edward softened somewhat at this view of the case, which was strongly urged by others of his nobles. So, by way of mending matters, he dismissed Sir Walter with his last requisition, which was, that six of the principal citizens of Calais, carrying the keys of the town and castle, should present themselves before him, bare-headed, bare-foot, and with ropes round their necks, and that he should do what he pleased with them; hang them, or not, as the humour took him; the rest of the inhabitants being permitted to go free.

It was a hard measure, but there was no help for it; and back went that generous soul de Manny with this last proposal, of which, no doubt, he was a little ashamed. On his arrival, the governor caused the town's bell to be rung, collected all the citizens in the public hall, and then communicated to them the final answer of the inplacable monarch. Loud lamentations and wailings broke forth from the assembled throng when the king's will was made known to them; and even the hardy knight de Vienne, wept at the sight of their distress. For awhile there was a gloomy silence throughout the multitude: life was sweet, and each one feared to lose it. At length patriotism, and a sense of duty prevailed even over the love of life; and one of the richest merchants of Calais, named Eustace de St. Pierre, rose up, saying, "Sirs, it would be great pity to suffer so many people to die of famine, if by any means it could be prevented, and it would be well-pleasing in the eyes of our Saviour, if such misery could be averted. I have such faith and trust in finding grace with God if I die to save my townsmen, that I offer myself as first of the six."

Bravely spoken Eustace de St. Pierre! That man's name deserves to come down to posterity.

As for the assembled crowd, they rose up, and as an old writer tells us, "almost worshipped him;" many throwing themselves, weeping, at his feet.

Another citizen, also wealthy and in great repute with his fellow townsmen, then offered himself to be the second. This was John Daire. Others followed, till the required number was complete; and Eustace de St. Pierre, John Daire, James and Peter Wisant, and two more whose names have perished, though the memory of their heroic deed endures, agreed to give themselves up to death to save the lives of the famish- ing people of Calais. The six were merchants, members of a class little esteemed by the knighthood of that day. But, merchants though they were, they were indeed *noble men*.

John de Vienne then collecting together his little

sacrificial band, mounted a small pony, (for his wounds disabled him from walking), and conducted them in the prescribed humiliating manner—bare-foot, bare-headed, and with ropes round their necks—to that gate of the town which opened on the English camp. A crowd followed them to the gate, weeping and lamenting· and when it was opened, the seven passed through to the English barriers, where Sir Walter Manny was waiting to receive them. The six citizens were delivered up to him, in due form, with an earnest request that he would intercede with his sovereign for their lives; and then de Vienne, with a heavy heart, turned back again to the miserable town.

When brought into Edward's presence, the prisoners, upon their knees, gave up the keys of the castle and town, praying the king to spare their lives. This, Edward at first did not seem at all disposed to do; the people of Calais had done him so much mischief by sea in times past, that he was now quite in a mood to cut off a few of their heads, by way of punishing them for it. And, accordingly, spite of the pitying looks and entreaties of the great lords and knights around him, he straightway gave command that the heads of the six should be stricken off. It was in vain his gallant followers interceded for the voluntary captives; he would not hear a word on their behalf. De Manny, and even the prince himself pleaded unavailingly, though they reminded him that a charge of cruelty, such as no true knight ought to incur, would certainly rest upon him, if he carried out his fierce purpose.

What was denied to the entreaties and remonstrances of his son, and of his nobles, Edward was, however, forced to grant to the prayers of his queen whom he tenderly loved, and who, having just crossed the seas to join him, after her victorious encounter at Neville's Cross, deserved some boon at his hands. On her knees, weeping, she prayed him for Christ's sake, as well as for his love to her, to have pity on these unfortunate citizens of Calais.

The king for awhile, and in silence, looked at the weeping, kneeling figure; and then gently telling Philippa he wished she had been anywhere, rather than where she was at that moment, for he could not refuse her request, bade her do with the six as she pleased. Nothing loth, she carried them off in triumph to her own tent, had those horrible ropes taken from their necks, clothed and fed them; and then, with a supply of money for their journey, commanded them to be safely conducted out of the camp.

It was in August 1347, after an eleven months' siege, that the strong town of Calais surrendered to the king of England. Edward, accompanied by his queen and son, took possession of it in state, having first ordered his officers to imprison a portion of the garrison, and drive all the inhabitants bodily out of the town, which he was resolved to convert into a thoroughly English one, by filling it with his own subjects. The king made Calais his residence for some little time, during which the prince, at the head of a strong detachment, made a sort of foray into the neighbouring country, which he burned and ravaged as far as the Somme, and then returned laden with spoil.

After this, as the one kingdom found fighting ruinous, and the other found it costly, a truce was agreed upon between the two; and Edward, having appointed a favourite Italian knight of his, named Sir Americ de Pavie, governor of Calais, set sail for England with the queen, the prince, and his little daughter Margaret, who had been born in the captured city. After being well tossed about on his own seas (he complained that winds and seas always favoured him when he went to France, but were dead against him on his return), he landed at Sandwich, then a considerable port, on the 28th of September.

Sir Americ de Pavie, the newly appointed governor of Calais, happened to be something of a rascal; and we shall hear of him again.

VI

Treachery at Calais.

THE young Prince of Wales was now a youth of seventeen; tall, handsome, strong, valiant, distinguished for his deeds of arms, as well as for the other knightly qualities of courtesy, moderation, and gentleness. He, and his illustrious parents, were received with acclamations by the English people, whose heads were nearly turned by those wonderful doings in France. In great state the three entered the city of London—for at that date, the city was a "genteel" place, and not as now, wholly given up to merchandise. Merchants, tradesmen, and artisans certainly exercised each one his calling, or craft there. But there also the great nobles had their dwellings, whose faded splendours may still be discerned in the warehouses and offices of modern times; bales of goods crowding the halls within which lords and ladies were wont to show their stately presence, and brisk clerks, scribbling away as if for their very lives, in the room of those who wielded the sword—the *power* of those days—and cased their limbs in steel, instead of broad cloth.

Royal feastings and tournaments celebrated the recent prowess of the new-made royal knight. And that young, muscular form, and stout heart distinguished itself in this mimicry of war, as it had done in the grim reality of it in France.

The tournament was the chosen diversion of knights and ladies of the fourteenth century. In it, companies of knights, armed as if for battle, save that lance and sword were pointless, spurred furiously against each other, squadron against squadron, till broken lances, knights unhelmed, or some of them lifted bodily out of their saddles by the shock, terminated the contest, and the one or the other was proclaimed victor. The ground enclosed for the purpose was called the lists; and it was surrounded by galleries for spectators, among whom ladies were conspicuous; for they as well loved to look upon these rough trials of skill, as the combatants themselves loved to enter upon them. Occasionally the excitement of these warlike games became so great that battle in play was converted into battle in downright earnest; and men were maimed, and lives lost within the gaily decorated lists, and under the unshrinking eyes of the high born dames surrounding them.

If only two knights engaged, the one against the other, it was called a joust.

At Canterbury, then a city of more importance than

(3)   6

it is now, and Eltham, where at that time stood a royal
palace, whose great hall has long ago been turned into
a barn, these festivities were held in notable style.
People's notions about being handsomely dressed vary
at different times and different places.   Here, at
Eltham, the extraordinary equipments of two of the
knights who levelled lance at each other, have been
handed down to us by admiring chroniclers; and
when we read in their dusky pages that over the
armour of these same cavaliers—armour, no doubt, of
most exquisite finish, after the fashion of tilting
armour—they wore hoods of white cloth, buttoned
with large pearls, and embroidered with figures of
dancing-men dressed in blue, we must admit that they
were magnificent according to their notions, and
supremely ridiculous according to ours.   *We* should
dress up a Merry Andrew in such guise.   With them
it was the sumptuous apparel of noble and gallant
soldiers; and for this special piece of finery the two
gentlemen, we are told, were indebted to the king's
wardrobe.   Five centuries hence, perhaps the people
of England may laugh at our modern notions of how
nobles and warriors should be habited.

Rejoicings and festivities, however, were not to last
long.   The stalwart youth upon whom the affection of
all England rested was to have more work—real work,
not pretence—found for him through the medium of
Sir Aymeric de Pavia, who, it has been said, was some-

thing of a rascal; and being one, soon showed him-self.

There was a French knight, Sir Geoffrey de Chargny, in command of St. Omer, who was what in England would have been called Lord Warden of the Marches. He was charged with the protection of the French frontier, and with the duty of keeping a sharp eye on the doings of their troublesome English neighbours in the north. Now, as old chroniclers tell us, this Sir Geoffrey bethought him that Lombards were not only poor, but money-loving; and as de Pavia was a Lombard, this consideration suggested how he should be dealt with for the interest of Philip of Valois. So Sir Geoffrey entered into communication with the Italian governor of Calais, and by degrees—we know not how he went to work—succeeded in persuading that honourable knight to sell Calais to him for twenty thousand crowns—about £10,000 of our money. It was a shabby transaction, but the story is quite true. A man high in command agreed to give up his trust to the enemy, in return for a sum of money! The affair was so snugly arranged, that it was thought no one could possibly know anything about it, and that the abominable bit of treachery would be consummated in perfect safety.

It was not so. King Edward loved and trusted the Lombard, but still took measures for ascertaining whether his affection and confidence were well bestowed;

and so it came to his ears how the town of Calais, the winning of which had cost him so dear, was to be sold to its former owners by the governor whom he had placed over it.

Sir Geoffrey and Sir Aymeric were a couple of clever fellows, but Edward was a match for them both. He at once despatched a messenger to Sir Aymeric, desiring him to come over to Westminster immediately —a command that was cheerfully obeyed, for it never entered the Italian's head that his roguery had been found out by his master. Doubtless he fancied some fresh mark of royal favour was about to be bestowed upon him! On presenting himself before the king, he was coolly informed of his treachery, and that he deserved to die for it. Down on his knees dropped the astounded knight, praying for mercy, assuring Edward there was plenty of time even yet for him to break faith with Sir Geoffrey, and earnestly begging that he might be allowed to expiate one act of treachery by another. The king was disposed to make use of him; the fellow had still the power of being serviceable; and therefore, instead of hanging him for his vile huckstering about the city of Calais, sent him back again, with full instructions how to undo what he had already done in the matter.

Only too happy this time to take in his friend Sir Geoffrey, in place of the King of England whom he had failed to entrap, the baffled Italian returned to his

governorship—not saying one word, good, bad, or in-
different, to the knight of St. Omer, who thereupon
thought all was right, and took his measures accordingly.

The time for the completion of the treason was at
length fixed. It was to be the last night of the year,
1348, and Sir Aymeric immediately sent his brother over
to England to tell the king.

Upon receipt of this news, Edward, who was keeping Christmas gaily at the queen's palace of Havering
in Essex, collected a small force of three hundred men-
at-arms and three thousand archers, and embarking
with them and the prince at Dover, got into Calais so
quietly, that no one except a few of his principal
officers knew anything about it. It was his will that
de Manny should have command of the enterprise—
king and prince, in plain armour to conceal their rank,
both fighting under him. The soldiers were placed in
ambuscade in different parts of the castle; and then
all was ready for Sir Geoffrey when he came with his
money.

Sir Geoffrey accordingly, on the 31st of December,
approached the town about midnight, having a good
force with him; and then halting to let his rear come
up, sent forward two of his squires to ask Sir Aymeric
if it were time for their master to advance. The Italian
said that it was; and immediately on hearing this, Sir
Geoffrey marched his men in battle array over the

bridge of Neuillet, sending forward twelve of his knights
with a hundred men-at-arms, to take possession of the
castle—for he thought that if he had that, the town
would easily follow. To one of these knights, Sir
Odoart de Renty, was entrusted the price of the town
and castle, as agreed upon with the governor.

The little party plodded on in the dark, till they
reached the castle, where the accommodating de Pavia
had already let down the draw-bridge for them; and
after they had passed over, Sir Odoart gave him the
bag of money. De Pavia took it, and, saying "he
had not time to count it, but supposed it was all
there," flung it into a room, which he immediately
locked up, telling the Frenchmen he would lead them
to the great tower that they might the sooner be masters of the castle.

The wicked Italian! In that very tower were the
king and prince, with two hundred followers, who, the
moment de Pavia pushed back the bolt, rushed out
upon the bewildered French, with the cry, "de Manny
to the rescue! What! do these Frenchmen think to
take the Castle of Calais with a handful of men?"
And with that they laid about them with their swords
and battle-axes in such a style as speedily satisfied
their French friends that now was the time for discretion rather than valour. Resistance was evidently
useless, so they at once yielded themselves prisoners.
They were politely handed into the tower whence the

English had issued; the key was turned upon them; and, leaving them strongly guarded, the English cavaliers sprang upon their horses, and sallied forth to find Sir Geoffrey.

Sir Geoffrey had drawn up the remainder of his little army in the plain, and there awaited the signal to advance and take possession. He was in a fidget: those twenty thousand crowns already handed over to the treacherous Italian, and yet no gates thrown open for him to march into Calais, as agreed upon! Sir Geoffrey was fidgetty; he was also cross, grumbling out to one near him that if the Italian were " much longer about opening the gate, they should all die of cold." And, indeed to stand thus in their ranks, mounted and under arms, in the middle of a December night, was a freezing sort of thing. The knight to whom he spoke answered sneeringly, that as the Lombards were a strange people, possibly Sir Aymeric was all this time counting the money, and examining it lest there should be any bad coin among it. Cold and vexed, of course both were rather spiteful. And yet they did not think half badly enough of Sir Aymeric de Pavia.

Vexed they were destined to remain, but not cold; warm work was at hand in place of freezing in their saddles. The two Edwards, with barons, and knights, and fluttering banners, were advancing in the grey morning, and with shouts of "Manny to the rescue!"

suddenly presented themselves to the enemy. "If we
fly," exclaimed Sir Geoffrey at this sight, "all is lost!
Let us fight it out!" "By St. George, you are right,"
replied some of the English who were near enough to
overhear him; "shame upon him who thinks of retreating!"

There was nothing for it now but to accept the
challenge thus given; and the two parties prepared to
do their best and worst at each other. Sir Geoffrey
placed his men a little in the rear of his first position;
and dismounting, that the battle might be on foot, they
drove their horses out of the way. They then planted
themselves in close order, with their lances, shortened
to five feet, held in such a manner as to present a
phalanx of sharp points towards the enemy. The
English were also on foot—king and prince under
de Manny's banner; and the contest was fierce between these two gallant companies. How the prince
fared we know not; but the king, we are told, matched
himself with a brave French knight, Eustace de Ribeaumont, who twice struck him down on his knees, but
was at last forced to surrender to the king, of whose
rank he was utterly ignorant. The English were
victorious in all directions. Such of the Frenchmen
as could catch their horses, rode off as fast as they
could, out-distancing the English, who had only their
own legs on which to pursue them; and Sir Geoffrey
de Chargny ended this little business of buying Calais

from its untrustworthy governor, by being himself, along with many others, carried prisoner within the walls which he had expected to enter as lord and master.

Not till they were brought into the presence of their captors did the Frenchmen know to what illustrious foes they had been opposed. Those two simple knights, under the well-known de Manny, were actually the English king and his son, who most courteously received their crest-fallen and unwilling visitors. As it was New Year's-day, the king would have them all to supper with himself; when, like a good host, he contrived to make them enjoy themselves, notwithstanding the disasters of the night. The French knights were his guests, and sat at the royal table. They were waited upon by the prince and his English knights, who afterwards quietly got their own supper at another table.

The king had a kindly word for every one except poor Sir Geoffrey, in whose teeth he could not help flinging, how that he had thought to get Calais more cheaply than it had been bought, and how he had been disappointed of it. To Sir Eustace, who had fought him more hardly, as he said, than any other knight with whom he had ever contended, he gave a rare circlet of pearls, and as much praise as that gallant gentleman could conveniently swallow. And so all ended politely, if not agreeably to some of the parties concerned.

Sir Aymeric was of course displaced from the office which he had so unworthily occupied; the governorship of Calais was bestowed upon Sir John Beauchamp, and the king and prince then returned to England.

But it was not to rest that the warlike king, and his son, growing up in his father's warlike image, came back again to their own island :—

" Fair jewel, in bright silver set ! "

Fighting, fighting, fighting was the order of the day five centuries ago; and after having fought and beaten the French, they had to fight and beat the Spaniards. To do the former the Black Prince and his father had had to go to France. The Spaniards came to them to fight, and be beaten signally.

It was in 1350, the year but one after that false Italian and scheming Frenchman had conspired to cheat Edward out of his dearly-bought acquisition of Calais, that the Spaniards thought proper to come and try the metal of the English in their own seas. They had better have stayed at home. We English consider the seas circling our island as our very own, and on this occasion we proved them so to the utter discomfiture of the invaders. The Spaniards came, sailing confidently enough, perhaps it should be said impertinently enough, along the Sussex coast, until what came of it was distinctly visible, the day being clear, from the hilly sea-side margin of that county.

The Spaniards had forty large ships, laden not only with merchandise from Flanders, but with more offensive stores in the shape of cannon and cross-bows, with ammunition to match, for the benefit of the English. Large stones and bars of beaten iron were also among their missiles, for the purpose of being pitched into vessels alongside to sink them. A similar plan is still occasionally adopted in modern naval warfare; *cold shot*, as it is called,—that is, balls heaved overboard instead of being discharged from a gun,—being thrown into small boats, with this design.

The king, being tired of the mischief done by the Spaniards to his merchant vessels, had made up his mind once for all to put an end to it. His design was seconded with all their hearts by his lords and other great men, so that a handsome fleet was readily equipped, and kept cruising between Dover and Calais to catch the Spaniards as soon as they made their appearance. The Prince of Wales commanded one division of the fleet. His young brother, the Earl of Richmond, afterwards known as the celebrated John of Gaunt, was also on board. Not that a lad of nine years old could be of any use, but that he was such a pet with his father that he would have him.

They had not to wait long for the Spaniards, and when they met, the appetite for hard fighting was equally good on both sides. The king immediately ordered his ship to be laid alongside the first Spaniard that bore down upon them. The two came together with a crash that broke the Spaniard's mast, and canted out of its upper works those who were stationed aloft to hurl down the large stones and iron bars spoken of; while at the same time the force of the concussion cracked the English vessel like a walnut, causing her to leak till she was near sinking. But for all that the two crews fought madly, and the English, leaving their own sinking ship, scrambled on the deck of the Spaniard, whose crew they threw overboard.

The prince and his division had their hands equally full elsewhere, for it was no ignoble foe to whom they were opposed. A huge hulk of a Spaniard came down upon his vessel, and grappling it fast, knocked them about to some purpose. The storm of cross-bow bolts, stones, and lumps of iron raged there, as it had done upon the king's ship, and as stoutly was it met; but meanwhile, between the straining timbers water poured in at such a rate that it was almost more than the crew could do, by incessant baling, to keep themselves afloat. They fought the more desperately for this, for it was—Conquer, or be drowned! At last they were rescued from inevitable destruction by the Duke of Lancaster, who, seeing the prince's extreme danger, made his vessel fast to the other side of the Spaniard, so as to hug her between them, and effected a diversion by the fierceness of this new attack. Two to one prevailed; the Spaniard struck his flag, and the prince, with his followers, climbing up her tall sides from their own sinking tub of a boat, which instantly went down, took possession, flinging the crew, to a man, into the sea : perhaps by way of expressing thankfulness for their own preservation! We don't do such things now-a-days.

Throughout the whole fleet the battle raged horribly for some hours, but victory eventually declared for the English. Fourteen Spanish vessels were sunk or taken, the rest sheered off, and then the battered English flotilla came to anchor about dusk between Rye and Winchelsea. Thence the king and his two sons hastened to the monastery where Queen Philippa had spent that anxious day, tormented by reports from her household, who, posting themselves on the hills overlooking the watery battle-field, conveyed to her most alarming accounts of the number and size of the enemy's ships. She was greatly comforted by seeing the two Edwards and her boy, who had "smelled powder" for the first time, all safe and sound. And feasting and merriment succeeded to the din of battle and the despairing cry of drowning Spaniards.

In this same year occurred an entertaining instance of the high esteem in which the King of England was held by foreign powers. Two knights, an Italian, John de Visconti, and a Frenchman, Sir Thomas de la Marche, fighting under the banner of the Kings of Armenia and Cyprus, against the Turks, had a violent quarrel. Vis-

conti accused de la Marche of taking a bribe to betray
the Christian army into the hands of its infidel enemies.
De la Marche told him that he lied; and as after this
there was nothing for it but a duel between them, it
was decided by their friends that the two should come
over to England to refer the matter to Edward as the
most heroic and honourable monarch in Christendom,
and, after the manner of the times, to fight a solemn
duel before him, the result of which was supposed to
prove the guilt or innocence of the accused party.

Visconti and de la Marche accordingly sailed to
England, and presenting themselves before the king,
delivered to him letters (signed by their royal and
noble leaders in the crusade), in which was set forth
the ground of their dispute, and that further prayed
him to suffer the two knights to settle it by single
combat before him. After delivering these letters,
Visconti formally accused de la Marche of the de-
grading treason mentioned in them, and threw down
his gauntlet in token of willingness to prove his accu-
sation by force of arms. De la Marche as stoutly took
it up, to signify his readiness to prove his innocence
in the same manner.

The king accepted the office of umpire between them,
and appointed a day whereon, at Westminster, the
cause should be thus strangely tried before himself,
the prince, and the whole court. At the time fixed the
combatants made their appearance, mounted and in

complete armour. The trumpets sounded for the charge, and they spurred their coursers against each other with all the vehemence of men who have given and received the lie; but both spears being broken in the first encounter without either of the knights being unhorsed, they sprang from their saddles and renewed the combat on foot with their swords. They struck hard and long until these at last were useless, and then, like a couple of tiger-cats, they flew at each other with their hands and arms, tugging and wrestling, till down they both tumbled in the lists. They might have kicked and struggled, and rolled over on the ground long enough, cased as they were in steel, had not de la Marche furnished himself with weapons that gave him what to our notions, seems a shabby advantage over his adversary. The joints of his gauntlets had sharp spikes, called gadlings, fixed in them, and striking these between the bars of his antagonist's helmet, Visconti, who had trusted, like a gentleman, to the ordinary weapons of such combats, was obliged to cry out for mercy, and own himself vanquished. The king upon this, throwing down his warder, proclaimed that the fight was at an end, and as de la Marche was victor, adjudged him guiltless of the crime laid to his charge.

The successful knight, who did not feel at all ashamed of the manner in which he had gained his victory (for, even in those chivalrous days, such things were permitted by the law of arms), then made a donation of his vanquished foe, who was his prisoner, to the prince, to be dealt with as he pleased. As we might expect, the captive was instantly liberated, and after receiving kindly courtesies from his owner, was permitted to return home at his leisure.

De la Marche further, in all the pride of proved innocence, dedicated his suit of mail (gadlings included, we suppose) to St. George, the patron saint of England, and devoutly hung it up in St. Paul's Cathedral for the acceptance of that mythological personage.

His venturing to try this cause in presence of the King of England, instead of settling it at home, is said to have cost him his life after his return to his own country.

It was amid the rejoicings after Edward's return from Calais that our English Order of the Garter was instituted by that monarch; the Black Prince being one of its first, and most illustrious knights.

VII.

The Prince's Expedition from Bordeaux.

PHILIP of Valois died on the 22d of August 1350, a few days before Edward's naval victory over the Spaniards, and was succeeded by his son John, a prince of many virtues, but not a particularly clever king. The truce between the two kingdoms still continued in name, but it was perpetually broken in little paltry ways, or smart skirmishes. In truth, the English and French did not love each other; at all events, not when the English were on French ground; and they could not help flying at each other whenever they came in contact. Perhaps, had each stayed on his own side of the channel, they might have been the best friends in the world. The English complained that the French broke the truce, and doubtless the French brought the same charge against the English. Being ourselves English, we are inclined to believe that we *did* keep it a little better than they. Indeed historians tell us that at this period Edward was sincerely desirous of being at peace with his neighbours.

But though Edward offered to resign his claim on the French crown provided he might hold his paternal possessions in that country free from the customary homage and also retain his much prized conquest of Calais, John resolutely declined to bargain with him on those terms.

In consequence of this, early in 1355, as the truce was to expire that year, the English king made vigorous preparations for setting to work again so soon as his engagement to be quiet had come to an end. His parliament, as usual, were liberal in finding him money for so popular a war; and the Prince of Wales, now in his twenty-fifth year, was sent into the west of England to rouse the martial ardour of the gentry and commonalty of that part of the country. This was done so effectually that, on the 10th of September, he sailed from Plymouth with a fleet of three hundred sail, having on board a gallant array of lords and knights, with their numerous retainers,—a force that, on his arrival at Bordeaux, was swelled by the enthusiastic natives of the English province of Guienne to the number of sixty thousand. Certainly here were—

" Enough to fight, enough to fall, and enough to run away."

Hitherto the fortunes of the Black Prince and his father have been so mingled that, following the one, we have of necessity followed the other. Now the independent action of the prince began, and we shall see what he could do alone.

The short autumn was spent in ravaging Languedoc, —a southern province containing more than half-a-dozen of the present departments of France,—burning, destroying, and making great numbers of prisoners, notwithstanding the presence in the province of a much larger French army, who appeared to think it best to let the prince have his own way.   Five hundred villages are said to have been burned during this foray, beside many fortified towns, before the prince thought fit to retire to winter quarters.   His father was busy doing similar mischief in the north of France, where King John was, like his army in the south, engaged in watching him, till Edward found it expedient to go home and defend his own territories against the Scots.

The summer of the coming year, 1356, was destined to see more important results, achieved too with a far smaller force.   On the 6th of July the prince left Bordeaux, the seat of his government, with a small army of two thousand men-at-arms and six thousand archers, only a part of whom were English, and penetrating the centre of France in a north-easterly direction, ravaged the country in a most awful manner. For some time, strangely enough, as before, there was no one to oppose him, and plunder and destruction went on at his pleasure.   Whenever that desperate

band of English and Gascons entered a well-provisioned
town, there they took their ease for a few days, and
when they departed, that no one else might do the
same, they destroyed all the food and drink that was
left.   O what a scene was there, over and over again,
of wheat and oats burning, wine casks dashed to pieces,
their contents streaming in all directions, and other
wreck and waste of God's good gifts to his thankless
creatures !   Of course the embarrassment of the enemy
is the object of all such dreadful work as this, which
still finds a place in our own wars, and *perhaps* it may
be needful to use even such means of preventing battles
having to be fought twice over.   But there is something
very shocking in wilful destruction of the fruits of the
earth, produced as they are by long toil and patience of
the husbandman, with God's blessing upon it, and whose
reproduction must require at least another twelve-
months' toil and patience.   Pulling down houses and
castles seems a trifle in comparison.   They are man's
work.   The fruits of the earth are peculiarly God's
work, for we might dig and delve till we were tired,
and yet never have a blade of corn did not He give it.

Vierzon, in the ancient province of Berri, now divided
into the departments of Cher and Indre, was the limit
of this terrible expedition; for while stopping there to
take breath, news was brought to the prince of the
French king's being ready for him at Chartres, about
sixty miles to the north of him, with an army at least

six times the size of his own. Further advance was impossible, as, in order to get at the French king (even had it been discreet to fight him), the English would have been obliged to cross the Loire, whose various passes were so strongly guarded that it was out of the question to think of forcing them. In such a state of things, going back again was the only course to be pursued. A council of war held by the prince, decided that this should be done; and, after wrecking and ruining Vierzon—for which they had no further use—the English and Gascons wheeled round, and set out on their return-march to Bordeaux.

The retreat—for so it must be called—was conducted in so orderly a manner, that for six days a French force of three hundred lances (that included a much greater number of men) hung upon their heels, without finding a chance of attacking them. This was disappointing; so, on drawing near the town of Romorantin, the Frenchmen took a roundabout course which placed them in advance of the English, for whom they then waited in ambuscade, in a spot commanding a very narrow pass through which the latter must proceed to reach the town. That very day, a company of two hundred horsemen, under some of the most distinguished lords and knights in the prince's army, had pushed forward before the main body, and coming up to this pass, rode safely through it. The moment that they had cleared it, however, the

French, who were well mounted, struck spurs into
their horses, and galloped after them, lance in hand.
The English, hearing the ring of the horses' hoofs,
turned round and instantly halted to receive the foe.
They opened their ranks as they did so, and the
French, charging full speed, dashed through them,
overturning not more than five or six of the English.
As soon as that whirlwind of men and horses had passed
through, the ranks were closed up, and, charging in
their turn, the English did terrible damage to the
French rear.　Down went knights, and squires, and
common men under the impetuous shock, and hand to
hand the two companies fought, till it was long uncer-
tain to which side victory would incline.　At this
juncture the vanguard of the English army came in
sight, skirting a wood; and then the French retreated
full speed, closely followed by the English troop, who
pursued them with much slaughter into the town of
Romorantin.　Of it they took easy possession, while
the pursued got safe into the castle, where they shut
themselves up.

　　The prince himself arrived in time to find how brisk
an encounter his little squadron had sustained; and
when he entered the town he found it crowded with
his own people, all anxious to attack the castle.　He
at once sent Sir John Chandos to hold a parley with
those who commanded in it.　These were a knight belonging to the neighbourhood, and an ecclesiastic; for

clergymen in those days were sometimes as clever in military science as in theology. Sir John accordingly advanced to the barriers, and making signs that he wished to speak to some one, the lord of Boucicault, and the hermit of Chaumont, came to meet him. Sir John, with all courtesy, then delivered the prince's message, which was to require the surrender of the castle, promising in that case, good terms to its garrison.

The lord of Boucicault and his clerical friend replied to Sir John that they were not at all disposed to accept his master's invitation to surrender ; nay, that they had made up their minds to fight it out to the last, if he thought proper to attack them. This was explicit, and Sir John Chandos and the Frenchmen returned to their respective quarters, little the better for their conference at the barriers.

The prince meant to have the castle, and hearing the ill success of his envoy in persuading its defenders to give it up, prepared to take it. Next morning a general assault was made upon the fortress, the English archers, like riflemen, being stationed in the ditches, and delivering their shafts with such precision that scarce a man dared to show himself upon the walls. Then, upon hurdles, and doors hastily torn down, anything in short, that would float, others eagerly crossed the ditch, and began undermining the walls with pickaxes and mattocks, heedless of the huge stones and pots of hot lime flung down upon them by the besieged. In this manner for a whole day the fierce work went on, without any decided advantage on either side, until night for a while separated the combatants. The English then retired to snatch a few hours' sleep, which might recruit them for a fresh attack in the morning. This renewed attempt was headed by the prince in person, and was as stoutly made as it had been on the preceding day. Amid the storm of missiles one of the prince's squires was slain by a great stone hurled from the castle, and this only made him the more resolute to have the fortress, cost what it might.

Some of the wiser heads among that soldierly set at length began to think that lances and arrows had not much chance against stone walls. So they got up some of the clumsy engines of war used in those days; (O, how different from our Armstrong guns!) and from them, bullets, and, what was still worse, Greek fire—a terrible composition that burned quite as well under water as above it—was shot into the castle. It was soon in a blaze ; and, burned out, and smoked out, the only chance for its defenders was to yield themselves to their assailants. They surrendered accordingly on the 4th of September. Great numbers of the garrison were mercifully set at liberty by the prince, and after having pulled down the castle, he pursued his route, carrying with him a couple of lords and the hermit as his prisoners.

The taking of the castle of Romorantin was a spirited little affair, and doubtless put the English in heart for what was to follow ; for Poitiers, whose name has for five centuries past rung in our ears like the blast of a trumpet, was now close at hand.

The prince (as he had sworn " by the soul of his father," his most solemn oath !) had taken this same castle of Romorantin ; but he had lost some precious time in doing so—precious, at least, if he desired to keep out of the way of John of France, with his sixty thousand Frenchmen. That vast army, composed of the best blood and the best sinews in France, having poured across the Loire at various points, was now rapidly gaining upon him—a circumstance that the increasing scarcity of forage led the prince to suspect ; and it was needful to decide upon some course of action. Determined to know the worst, he sent out a detachment of sixty men, well armed and mounted, to look about for the enemy ; and these getting among some heath and wood in the neighbourhood, came by accident in sight of a small party of French who were straggling along that way to reach their main body. There were about two hundred of them, and as soon as their quick eyes had made out the English troop, they donned their helmets, unfurled their banners, and setting lance in rest, spurred after them. The English, having the prince so close behind, had a mind to let themselves be pursued, in order to draw the French .

into a trap. So they turned round, and made briskly for the rugged road that led through the wood. The invitation thus given was too tempting to be declined; and away after them clattered the whole squadron, shouting and hallooing, to what they supposed the fly-ing enemy, till all at once, in their headlong haste, they found themselves right upon the prince's own banner. The skirmish that ensued was very hot and fierce. Almost all the Frenchmen were either slain or taken prisoners; and from the latter the prince learned that the king of France, with his whole army, was so near at hand that it would be impossible to avoid a battle.

This was serious; but the spirit of the lion-hearted Plantagenet still glowed in the bosom of his descendant, and suitable preparations for the inevitable contest were immediately made. Stragglers were recalled, and com-manding, on pain of death, that none should break the ranks, whatever might be the temptation to a separate tilting match with the enemy, the prince that Saturday gave his men a seven hours' march before halting in the plains of Maupertuis, a few miles from Poitiers. Here, in a strong position, surrounded by vineyards and hedges—small, teezing, but very effectual obstacles in the way of the enemy's horse—he camped for the night.

The prince had no sooner halted his banners than he detached a squadron of two hundred well-mounted men-at-arms for the purpose of reconnoitring. This party was under the command of several knights, among whom was Sir John de Greilly, Captal de Buche, one of the great fighting men of those days. That title, Captal, was an old and very rare one of southern France, and is equivalent to the one of count. They soon came upon the rear of the French, whose horsemen were swarming over the plain, and, making a rush at them, knocked many out of their saddles, besides taking some prisoners. This attack upon their rear, threw the whole main body of the French into commotion; and news of it being carried to the king, he turned back from the city of Poitiers, which he was just entering, pitching his tents in the field instead. And very late indeed was it, we are told, before those startled Frenchmen got to bed that night!

The return of the captal and his companions made the prince fully aware of the danger of his situation, and the impossibility of escape. "God help us," was his exclamation after hearing their report, "then we must see how we may best fight them!"

The prince, however, knew that God helps those who help themselves, and he at once set about strengthening and fortifying the well-chosen position which he had taken up. His troops were posted, as has been said, on a little sloping plain surrounded by woods and vine-yards, hedges and ditches, and open to attack in front only. To reach them even that way the assailants must approach through a narrow lane, in which four horsemen could scarcely ride abreast. The hedges on each side this lane were now lined with archers, so that any troops entering would be placed between a cross fire of arrows—worse one thinks than a cross fire of rifles, for each of those keen arrow-heads had a yard-long tail attached to it, which must have added horribly to the pain and embarrassment of the poor wretches whose bodies were pierced by them. At the end of the lane, where it opened on the ground occupied by the English army,—if such a name as army may be given to a small body of eight or ten thousand men,—another company of archers was drawn up, and these were backed by dismounted men-at-arms. Behind these the remainder of this terribly inadequate force was disposed in three lines; the Earl of Warwic commanding the van, the prince himself heading the main body, while the Earls of Suffolk and Salisbury took care of the rear. A chosen body of troops, led by the captal, was sent, under cover of night, round a hill that stood to the prince's right in order to flank the enemy in case of an engagement. Such entrenchments as the nature of the ground permitted were rapidly thrown up: and thus he prepared to receive the French in the renowned battle of Poitiers.

The King of France had been no less busy ordering his huge battalions for the coming struggle. The English were few in number, but past experience told him they were not to be despised on that account.

Early next morning,—it was Sunday,—after prayers
in his tent, and receiving the Holy Communion with his
four sons, he also prepared for the battle by arranging
his army according to what we may call the "rule of
three,"—that is, in three divisions, like those of the
prince except in size, for each one of these contained
twice as many men as were in the whole English army.
The van was under the leadership of his brother, Philip
of Orleans, the main body was commanded by the
Dauphin, his eldest son, with whom were his brothers
Lewis and John, and some renowned commanders to
take care of the boys!   The rear was under the king
himself; his youngest son Philip, a boy of fourteen,
being with his father.   It was a fine sight, whether
under the rich rays of a September sun, or thrown into
dead dense masses by a lowering sky,—historians do not
tell us what kind of day it was,—and the innumerable
banners and pennons that flickered over the heads of
this mailed host proclaimed the presence of the noblest
chivalry of France.

While the army was being formed in order of battle,
the king sent Sir Eustace de Ribeaumont,—he who had
received the pearls from our Edward as the prize of
superior valour,—and some other knights to examine
how the English had disposed themselves.   During
their absence on this errand, he addressed his army,
reminding them how they had been in the habit of
boasting what they would do to the English if they

could only get at them, and that now, with the enemy in sight, was the time to make good their vaunts. This address was cheerfully responded to, thousands vowing that, with God's help, they would that day show themselves true men. At that moment up came Sir Eustace and his companions, who, after having informed the king of the numbers of the English army, and the excellent manner in which it was drawn up, advised that a body of three hundred of their own best armed and mounted gentlemen should first force the passage of the lane, and beat down the archers at the other end of it, and then that the battle should take place on foot; the entrenchments of the English and their natural fortifications of hedge and ditch being such as to impede the action of cavalry except in this first instance of clearing the way.

This advice was acted upon. The army was formed as for battle, each lord under his own banner; and all alike, knights, squires, and men-at-arms dismounted. They were ordered to take off their spurs, which might have tripped them up had they been left on their heels; and to shorten their lances to five feet that they might be the more manageable in close combat.

The two armies were on the point of engaging when a peace-maker appeared on the scene. The Pope had more than once endeavoured to settle the quarrel between the kings of France and England, and now by his mission, one of his cardinals, de Perigord, made a

fresh attempt to prevent bloodshed.   Coming full gallop to the king, as he stood there armed from head to
foot, he entreated him, for the love of God, to stay a
moment and suffer him to go to the prince with such
terms as might induce a brave man to retire from what
the French deemed a hopeless contest.

The king was impatient to begin the battle, but he
could not for very shame refuse this request of the
cardinal, who forthwith rode off to the English camp.
There, on foot, in the midst of a vineyard, he found the
prince, who most courteously received his visitor.   The
cardinal entreated that he might be permitted to make
peace between him and King John, and the prince replied that he would willingly listen to any reasonable
terms, such as would neither touch his own honour nor
injure his army.   For, with seven to one against him,
he thought it as much the part of a good general to
treat with the enemy as to lead on his slender force to
a heroic but most probably fatal contest.   Rashness
and bravery are two different things, though they are
sometimes confounded.   The prince was brave; hence,
seeing himself so vastly outnumbered by an army including all the greatest warriors of France, he was ready
to treat on honourable terms.   Had he been rash, he
would have insisted upon fighting without more ado.
Finding the prince thus disposed to an accommodation,
if it could be brought about, the cardinal ambled back
again, and prevailed upon the king to agree to a truce

till next morning in order to give opportunity for arranging a cessation of hostilities. He had some difficulty in persuading him to this, for, in truth, John wished the cardinal and his peace-making far enough!

All that Sunday did the good cardinal hurry backwards and forwards between the French and English armies, vainly urging these two princes to put fighting out of their heads. All his pains were fruitless, and that they were so was entirely the fault of King John, who fancied the English were so completely in his power that he might do as he pleased with them. The prince was so fully aware of his hazardous position that he even offered to give up all his conquests in the recent expedition, the castle of Romorantin included, to set free the whole of his prisoners without ransom, and further, to engage not to take up arms against France for the next seven years. But when John, in addition, insisted that the prince and one hundred of his knights should yield themselves his prisoners, else he *would* fight, the thing became preposterous; and indignantly declaring that his countrymen should never have to pay his ransom, the prince threw the whole negotiation overboard, and prepared to defend himself as he best could.

It was sad folly on John's part, as we shall see. He was just like the boy with the filberts; grasping too much, he lost all.

During the interval occupied by the cardinal's amiable

but unavailing exertions, various knights from the two armies rode out to have a look at the enemy, and criticize his plan of operations. Chandos on the one side and de Clermont on the other were among these, and meeting in the plain, a very amusing but very brisk little quarrel sprang up between them. As these two redoubted warriors drew near each other, they perceived, to their mutual disgust, that each had precisely the same coat of arms embroidered on his surcoat. Now, in those days, for one gentleman to assume the armorial bearings of another was considered about as deadly an offence as could possibly be given: accordingly de Clermont called out fiercely,—" Chandos, since how long is it that you have taken upon you to wear my arms ?" With equal fierceness Chandos retorted that it was de Clermont who had stolen his. This was met by a flat denial from the Frenchman; with the addition that, but for the truce existing between them, he would soon show, by force of arms, who had the best right to the disputed coat. Chandos, in return, angrily bade him prove that next day in the field; and when the Lord de Clermont had relieved his feelings by a sneer at the English, who, being unable to invent anything new, were always ready enough to help themselves to the " handsome" devices of their neighbours, the two knights parted in high dudgeon.

The Battle of Poitiers.

THE eventful morning came,—Monday, the 19th of September 1356,—that was to decide whether the English were to be swept out of France, or King John taught a lesson of moderation in dealing with a valiant enemy.

The prince, before engaging, briefly addressed his brave fellows, reminding them that though they were but a small company, yet victory depended, not upon numbers, but upon the will of God, Who gave it as He pleased. He therefore besought them, for God's sake, to do their best that day, as he, their prince, with God's help, would also do. And few as they were, that "small company" were in high spirits for the coming battle.

The specially well-armed and well-mounted body of French gentlemen, of whom we have already heard, began the attack by endeavouring to force the passage of the lane leading to the ground occupied by the English army. Their gallant steeds stalked statelily between the two hedges; but once fairly in, from both sides of the way came a shower of arrows, directed chiefly at the horses, that set them a-plunging and capering till their riders found it impossible to control them. Smarting with wounds, the frightened animals at last turned right round, jerking the heavily-armed knights and squires out of their saddles in all directions; those who were thrown being speedily trampled under foot. Some few spurred their horses over or through the hedges, and so came upon the archers posted at the end of the lane, by whom they were soon cut to pieces. Seeing the discomfiture of their cavalry, a large body of dismounted men-at-arms, under the two French marshals, de Clermont and d'Andreghen, threw themselves into that deadly lane, and for awhile pressed forward desperately. But they fell thick and fast under the snow-like storm of arrows (for the archers of Poitiers were those of Crecy) that flanked them, and such as struggled through, spent and disordered, were an easy prey to the English men-at-arms. One of their leaders was slain, d'Andreghen was taken prisoner, and finally the greater part were fairly beaten back, so that, pressing upon the troops behind, they not only impeded their advance, but frightened many so terribly that they ran off to their horses, and rode away as fast as they could.

Galled by a continued and thick flight of arrows, the entire first battalion of the French gave way. At this juncture the captal and his horse came thundering round the hill, and fell upon the division of the Dauphin; which, already in confusion through the rout of those in front, was thrown into utter disorder by this impetuous attack of cavalry, supported by archers, who, as an old chronicler tells us, " shot so thickly and well, that the French did not know which way to turn themselves to avoid their arrows." Seeing the battalion waver, the English, who had hitherto fought on foot, sprang on their horses, which were ready at hand, and led by the prince, dashed in among the Frenchmen with loud shouts of " St. George for Guienne." " Montjoye St. Denis," was the answering cry, as the ponderous mailed men and horses came clashing against each other, and were at once plunged into a very whirlwind of battle. The life-blood of many a lord, and knight, and squire that day streamed over the gay armour whose steel-plates were riven by stout English lance-thrusts, or those intolerable arrows. The Frenchmen were brave, no one doubted that, but somehow panic and fright got among them, and once in, there was no getting rid of it. The noble lords to whom King John had committed the guardianship of his three eldest sons, by way of taking care of the youths, discreetly ran away with them; and in their company galloped off eight hundred lances,—that is, as many knights, with their followers,—for whom the distant sight of the combat had been more than enough. Pell-mell, hither and thither rolled and raged that fearful battle, some flying, some fighting fiercely, but with horrible loss on the part of the French.

The third division, under the king, stood its ground better than the other two; and had all fought as did John himself, the defeat which his sixty thousand suffered from eight thousand would have been less crushing. But his personal valour, together with that of the spirited boy at his side and a devoted few who had gathered round them, could not retrieve the fortunes of that fatal day. Three hours' bloody work swept the French host off their own plains, leaving the Black Prince and his heroic few, undisputed masters of the field. Such a defeat seems inexplicable : and yet so it was; showing that victory, as the prince had said, is not a mere matter of numbers, but that it falls to those to whom God wills to give it.

It was indeed He who gave it to this handful of English and Gascons, who, the very day before, had been insultingly required to deliver up their best and bravest leaders as prisoners to the now vanquished enemy.

The battle seemed already at an end, and yet John, spite of wounds, and having lost his helmet in the struggle, was still dealing around him heavy strokes with his battle-axe, in a sort of despairing attempt to cut his way out of the throng of English and Gascons that were pressing around him, with loud shouts to

surrender "or he was a dead man." There was no
escape for him; and pulled to and fro by his eager
captors, he anxiously inquired for the Prince of Wales,
that he might give himself up to one of equal rank
with himself.   But the prince was in a distant part of
the field; and the king was at length compelled to
throw down his gauntlet, in token of surrender, to Sir
Denis de Morbeque, a French knight in the English
service, who had shouldered his way through the crowd
to get at him.

While this extraordinary scramble for a king was
taking place, the prince, worn out with heat and fatigue,
was implored by Sir John Chandos (who had never
left him the whole day, and whose practised eye saw
that the day was their own), to take breath and rest
awhile, now that his work was done.   That experienced
commander advised that the prince's banner should be
displayed on a little eminence at hand, to serve as a
rallying point for such of his forces as had been carried away in their wild pursuit of the flying enemy,
who were slaughtered up to the very gates of Poitiers.
This was done, and a tent being pitched, the prince
took off his helmet to cool himself, and pour some
wine down his parched throat, while trumpets and other
instruments of music rang out joyous notes of victory.
The number of knights around him was continually
increasing, as one and another returned from the chase
bringing his prisoners with him.   From some of these

the prince inquired whether anything was known of King John; and as none knew what had become of him, save that he was certainly killed or taken, as he had never quitted the field, the Earl of Warwic and Lord Cobham were sent to seek him out.

They immediately mounted their horses, and making for a small hillock, where they might overlook the whole plain, saw a crowd of dismounted men-at-arms coming slowly along, and evidently in great commotion. The unfortunate King of France and his son were the centre of this unruly group, and in no little danger from the over-anxiety of each one to make good his claim to so distinguished a prisoner. They pushed and pulled him about, bawling, "It was I that took him;" "No, no, it was I;" and some were ready brutally to settle the dispute, by killing the subject of their rude contention. The king entreated them to take him and his son courteously to the prince their master; assuring his rival captors that there was no need to quarrel about him, seeing he was able to enrich them all by his ransom. But they gave no heed to his remonstrances; the fellows could not take a step without breaking out into new brawls about their prisoners; and it was well that at this juncture Warwic and Cobham caught sight of the party. Conjecturing from their violent excitement, that they had got some one of importance, the two lords spurred among them in a moment, and asking what was the

matter, were told that they had captured the King of
France, and that more than ten knights and squires
were contending for him, each one protesting that the
king was his prisoner.

My Lords Warwic and Cobham settled that question
upon the spot. Pushing through the crowd, whom
they unceremoniously drove right and left, they commanded every one to keep his distance, on pain of
death; then, with all reverence, taking possession of
the king's person themselves, they respectfully conducted him to the prince.

During their absence on this errand, the prince's
next inquiry was about the Lord James Audley; one
of the most renowned of his knights, who, before the
battle began had earnestly requested that he might be
foremost in the attack, in compliance with a certain
vow which he had made; a thing not unusual in those
strange old days. His petition being granted, he
placed himself with his four squires, far in advance of
the first division of the army, to be ready for the
enemy. The names of these squires have come down
to us, and they deserve a place in our record. They
were Dutton of Dutton, Delves of Doddington, Fowle-
hurst of Crew, Hawkstone of Wainehill; perhaps even
after the lapse of five hundred years they may still
have descendants,—in blood, if not in name. This
little company did wonders that day, beating down all
before them, or chasing them off the field, without

stopping to make prisoners. Glory, which in this instance was self-defence, was their object; not gain, from large ransoms. Those who give hard blows, however, may chance to receive them, and the gallant Audley's headlong career at Poitiers was ended by wounds innumerable, which, before the close of the engagement, compelled his squires to drag him aside, strip off his armour, and be his surgeons to the best of their ability. All this was told the prince, and also that the wounded man was lying in a litter (a sort of hand carriage), hard by.

The good-natured prince, grieved to hear of the brave knight's condition, sent some of his people to see whether Audley were in a fit state to be brought to him; as, if he were not, he would himself go to him. A pleased and proud man was the bruised, battered, and slashed Lord James when this condescending message was brought him, and calling eight of his servants he bade them carry him, litter and all, to his master. The prince leaning over the wounded man, embraced and thanked him for his services, commending his prowess in terms of such princely graciousness as were more than a balm for the knight's aching wounds. Nor did he confine himself to praise alone ; on the spot he conferred upon his faithful friend a yearly pension of near £4000, of our present money ; a royal gift which the Lord James (after gratefully acknowledging it to the donor), subsequently bestowed .

upon his four squires, whose good swords had that day
helped him to win so much glory.

There was a strange simplicity about the fighting
men of those days. To ensure the validity of this gift
to his squires, the Lord Audley summoned several
English nobles, relations of his, to his tent; and in their
presence, whom he called upon to bear witness to it,
formally made the donation to the four. These stern
warriors were deeply moved by his generosity, and as
they glanced one at another, there broke from them
the response: "May the Lord God remember you for
this! We will bear witness to this gift whensoever
and wheresoever we may be called upon to do so."
The prince hearing afterwards that his grant had been
handed over to my lord's squires, was so far from being
offended, that he replaced the pension by one of much
larger amount.

Just as the wounded knight was being borne away,
Warwic and Cobham were seen approaching with their
royal prisoner. The prince went forth to meet them;
and when they met, bending as reverentially before
John, as though the king were still in the height of
his power, he conducted him to his tent, with such
soothing, kindly words as only the heart of a thorough
gentleman could, at such a moment, have prompted.
With his own hands he presented refreshments to the
discomfited and toil-worn monarch, in so amiable a
manner as could not but take off the sharp edge of his

sore calamity. There was no triumphing over a fallen foe, nor even wounding slight, of one who not twenty-four hours before had proposed such insolent terms to those whom he reckoned at his mercy, but in whose hands a sudden reverse had now placed his own fate. Had there been either the one or the other, scarce any could have wondered at it. But the young conqueror was master of *himself;* a mastery which some do not attain throughout a long life; and spite of temptations to the contrary, on this occasion fully carried out the golden rule : to do to others, as we would that they should do to us. John was touched by a generosity which he well knew how to appreciate; though, in the hour of his own fancied superiority, he had suffered himself to be carried away by feelings of an opposite nature; and in few, kingly, heartfelt words, paid to the prince's goodness and valour, the tribute they so well deserved.

There was now leisure to examine into the results of this famous Battle of Poitiers. 'It was crushing to the French. The chief of their nobility and knighthood were either slain or taken prisoners, thousands were lying dead on the plains of Maupertuis, while to crown their misfortunes their king himself, with his son, was in the hands of the victors. To the English it was deliverance from destruction, cheaply obtained, for, as before, their loss was inconsiderable. The prisoners that they had made outnumbered their own army two-

fold; so that, ere the day was over, the work of ransom
went briskly on.   Both English and Gascons were very
liberal in this matter, no larger ransom than a man
could conveniently pay being exacted from him, and
many were at once liberated on their own promise to
bring the amount agreed upon to Bordeaux the next
Christmas.   They could afford to be liberal, seeing their
prisoners were at the rate of two to a man.   And
further, those vain-glorious French, taking for granted
they were going to drive the English—to Jericho! had
come to the field as splendidly armed as though it
were to a tournament, and furnished as if for a festival.
So that, beside ransom money, vast quantities of
jewels, gold and silver plate, and rich holiday vest-
ments, fell to the share of their fortunate conquerors.
But there was more than liberality shown to the
prisoners on this occasion; there was kindly courtesy
also, for the humane conduct of the prince had its
influence upon every one under his command.   Doubtless also their own unlooked for escape from what
appeared inevitable ruin, had had its effects in soften-
ing their hearts.

Sir Denis de Morbeque, though he took a king, was
in danger of coming worse off than any of his companions, who had picked up more ignoble prey; for the
ransom of a king, in those days, was fixed at so large
a sum, that, according to the law of arms, no private
knight might receive it.   None but the rival sovereign

was allowed to pocket such illimitable cash. Sir
Denis, however, had great glory thereby, and in due
time a very satisfactory gift from his own prince, to
make amends for the ransom he had lost.

It was late in the evening before all the English
were collected in camp again, after their pursuit of the
enemy. Business being then ended, there was leisure
for refreshment, and the duties of hospitality. The
prince had a magnificent supper prepared in his own
tent, for the king, his son, and such of his nobles as
were of sufficient rank to partake in the entertainment.
The said supper was furnished out of the captured French
baggage-waggons; for, in addition to danger from the
enemy, the English had, the day before, been in some
risk of starving; food being so scarce in the camp,
that many of the poor fellows had scarcely tasted bread
for three days. No fear now of an empty larder! The
king and his son, with half-a-dozen of his very greatest
lords, were placed in state at a table a little higher
than those at which the rest of the captive company
were seated; and upon him the prince himself waited,
with all courtesy. His prisoner-guest would fain have
urged him to take a seat at his own table; but the
prince modestly declined doing so, saying he was not
worthy of the honour, of sitting down in the presence
of so puissant a monarch, and so valiant a knight, as
John had that day shown himself. He then prayed
the king not to make the worse cheer because God

had withheld victory from his arms; assuring him that from the King of England he would receive such honourable and friendly treatment, as would in all likelihood restore peace between the two kingdoms. And he delicately commended the bravery of the French king, while he endeavoured to console him under his misfortunes.

John was moved to tears by the generosity of his conqueror, and a murmur of applause arose from the French nobles, who declared, that if God gave him life, the young Englishman would be one of the most gallant princes in Christendom.

The next morning, after public thanksgivings for this signal victory, the camp was broken up, and the army, laden with spoil, and carrying with it the royal prisoners, resumed its march to Bordeaux. An advanced guard of five hundred men-at-arms preceded it to see that the way was clear, but such was the consternation spread throughout the country that none dared to oppose them. Their progress was slow, owing to the vast quantity of heavy baggage which they carried in their train; but Bordeaux was at last gained, and thrown into a tumult of joy by the prince's good fortune. The royal party took up their abode in the monastery of St. Andrew—the king and his son occupying one side, and the prince the other. There the winter was spent in much feasting and merriment; the English and Gascons throwing about them in all directions the gold they had so abundantly won at the battle of Poitiers.

The rejoicings in England were no less vivid, for indeed the prince's victory had laid the kingdom of France almost at Edward's feet. Solemn thanksgivings in churches, with bonfires in every town and village, testified the public joy; and such knights and squires as had been in that famous battle, held up their heads higher than ever when they returned to their native country.

Early in the spring of 1357, the prince prepared to leave Bordeaux for England, carrying King John and his son with him. But his Gascon lords were very unwilling to lose sight of so illustrious a prisoner, whom they had, as they said, helped to take; and they told the prince, quietly, that it was not their intention to permit his being taken away from them. The king—they thanked Heaven for it—was in excellent health, the city of Bordeaux was quite good enough for a royal residence, they felt themselves perfectly equal to keeping guard over him, and therefore it was their will that he should remain where he was. Things were taking an awkward turn now. Two or three dozen great barons making up their minds that they would *not* allow a certain thing to be done, was enough in the middle ages to make even a monarch hesitate. Possibly they might do now; but in those days they were apt to take rougher ways of carrying their point.

The prince had already sought to propitiate these gentlemen by deputing them to high and honourable offices in the province during his absence, as well as by promising them "great rewards and profits," which, as a malicious old writer remarks, "are all that a Gascon loves or desires;" and yet, like Oliver, they were "asking for more!" In reply, he politely admitted the cogency of what they had said, but added that the king his father had a strong desire to see so notable a prize of the late battle, and indeed to have possession of it himself! And again he thanked them for their loyal service, and promised them suitable rewards.

Neither flattery nor promises moved the sturdy Gascons from their purpose. At length Chandos and Cobham, who, being better acquainted with them than the prince was, knew at what these lords were aiming, whispered to him, "Sir, sir, offer them a handsome sum of money, and you will soon find they will do whatever you please." The prince took the hint, and proposed sixty thousand florins as the price of their submission. This was rejected; and as he perceived it was simply because he had not bid high enough, he raised his offer to one hundred thousand, which they thought proper to accept; giving him, in return, permission to set out on his travels as soon as he liked!

This important point settled, the prince and his prisoners took ship on the 24th of April. The fleet that conveyed them was large and strongly armed, for there were alarming reports of those well-beaten French having raised two large armies, and posted them so that they might readily fall upon the English as they sailed up the channel, and rescue the king. They proved mere reports, the only dangers of the voyage were those from weather, and all disembarked, safe and sound, at Sandwich on the 5th of May. Two days' rest was enjoyed here, and then the calvalcade took its slow way, by Canterbury, Rochester, and Dartford, to London, where, by the king's command, extraordinary preparations had been made to give the prince and his illustrious captives a fitting reception.

Never surely, either before or since, was Lord Mayor in such a turmoil and worry of anxiety as was Sir Henry Picard, who at that time filled an office of rather more importance than it is in our days. A Lord Mayor, five centuries ago, was somebody ; not as now, when he "stands, the shadow of a name ;" and Sir Henry had to pay the penalty of greatness. His cares and fatigues in doing the honours of his own domain, were, however, well rewarded by the success of the pageant got up by this zealous dignitary to dazzle the eyes of the fallen monarch, while it exhibited the wealth and greatness of his captors. At Southwark the prince and his train were met by a thousand citizens on horseback, dressed in their best, and by them conducted over London Bridge into the city ; John, robed as became a king, mounted on a magnifi-

cent white charger, while the prince, plainly apparelled,
ambled by his side, on a small black horse. On entering the city the throng of sight-loving Englishmen was
so great that they had some ado to make their way
through it; leaving them ample time to admire all the
fine things brought out by the inhabitants to do their
visitors and themselves honour—houses, shops, win-
dows, balconies, on either side were all a-glitter, not
only with plate and tapestry, but with the sterner wares
of arms and armour. Shields, helmets, corslets, breast
and back pieces, coats of mail, gauntlets, swords, spears,
bows and arrows, battle axes, and costly horse furniture
of polished mail, were displayed in picturesque profusion. And seven mortal hours were consumed in
passing along these decorated streets before the long
procession reached its journey's end. As it approached
Westminster a train of clergy, in the sumptuous robes
of that period, came forth to meet their prince, chant-
ing as they walked the solemn melodies of the Church.
And thus, accompanied by civil, military, and ecclesi-
astical dignities, the heir of England entered Westminster Hall, where his father, on a throne of state,
awaited him. Edward rose to receive his royal visitor
as though that reluctant visitor had been a friend
rather than a captive; and, after courteously saluting
him, embraced and thanked his son amid the thundering acclamations of the vast concourse around.

King John was that night royally entertained by his

brother of England, and then had the palace of the Savoy, a noble building belonging to the Duke of Lancaster, assigned to him and his son for their residence. The king and queen frequently visited them. It was not long afterwards exchanged for Edward's own palace of Windsor Castle, where John and Philip went about hunting, and hawking, and diverting themselves according to their tastes, very much as though they had been at home!

The English again Invade France.

THE kingdom of France was reduced to a most miserable condition by the fatal battle of Poitiers. Its monarch a captive, its noblest and most valiant slain,—all its affairs fell into the utmost confusion. The dauphin, a youth of eighteen, assumed the government, but he was too young to have much authority in such troublous times. Things were quite above his hand. So the chief of the remaining nobles, the clergy, and the citizens, met together at Paris, and decided that thirty-six of their number, chosen equally from each class, should govern the country in the absence of its king. But this government also was one that had little weight; and spite of it, disorder, misery, and bloodshed, filled the land.

In one department of France, the peasantry rose in insurrection with the avowed intention of killing all the nobility and gentry, whose use in the kingdom they professed themselves incapable of seeing. Having selected for their chief one whose pre-eminence in bad-ness had pointed him out for that distinction, they dubbed him Jacques Bon-homme, (a name whence this insurrection takes its title of the Jacquerie), and under his leadership they outrageously attacked the upper classes, purposing to exterminate every man of them. If it had been men alone upon whom they wreaked their vengeance, it would not have been so bad ; but these wretches also murdered women and children with incredible ferocity.   The horrid cruelties of which they were guilty make one's blood cold but to read of; and people fled before them in all directions, recklessly abandoning their fine houses and castles, with the rich and costly furniture of them, to the fury of the rebels ; too happy if themselves, with their wives and children, might escape with their lives : better be houseless and homeless than torn to pieces by such demons as were the followers of Jacques Bon-homme.   Among those who thus fled for their lives, were the Duchess of Normandy, and more than three hundred other ladies, who shut themselves up in the city of Meaux, under the protection of the Duke of Orleans.   They fancied they should be safe here, but would have found themselves wofully mistaken had it not been for the chivalrous gallantry of an enemy—the Captal de Buch, and his cousin, the Count of Foix—who, hearing of their distress, (for the people of Meaux had opened their gates to the rebels), hastened to the rescue.

The captal and his friend were only just in time—

nine thousand of the insurrectionary mob had marched upon the town, which they were entering, when these two good knights, with a slender retinue of horsemen, came upon them. They met in the market-place; and fearful, as well as deserved, was the execution done by sword and lance on the ill-armed, ferocious throng of peasants. They had shown no mercy, and assuredly now they found none. Dead and dying, they were flung into the river by wholesale, while those who fled were pursued and struck down until seven thousand of the nine were destroyed. This terrible vengeance put an end to the Jacquerie.

The Parisians, under their provost, had also taken advantage of the distresses of their country to get up a revolt in the capital itself, and no little trouble did its suppression cost the unfortunate Duke of Normandy.

All these things made the French still more desirous that peace should be concluded between them and the English.

A truce (that is, a cessation of hostilities) for three years had indeed been agreed upon during the time King John was at Bordeaux; and that gave both parties time to think over the matter, and consider whether they might not do better than continue working each other all the mischief in their power. King John, however, had been in captivity nearly three years before a treaty of peace could be arranged. At length, a few months before the expiration of the truce, he and

the Lord James de Bourbon, one of his nobles, together
with King Edward and the Prince of Wales, proposed
certain terms of peace, including three hundred thousand crowns for the king's ransom, and one million for
that of his nobles who were prisoners with him; Edward, on his part, engaging in return to renounce his
claim to the French crown.   This treaty was sent over
to the dauphin for his acceptance; but, acting by the
advice of his council, that young prince rejected it.
They said the terms were too hard, and that, rather
than submit to them, they would not only endure the
distress in which they then were, but leave their king
to his fate.

King John was not particularly pleased with this
answer.   In it he thought he detected the influence of
his old enemy the King of Navarre, whom the dauphin,
in his distraction, had taken into his confidence, and
whom John knew to be capable of deceiving forty such
innocent youths as his eldest son.   As for King Edward,—why, as the French declined the peace he offered
them, he at once prepared to go to war with them more
formidably than ever.

Meanwhile, that pleasure might go hand in hand
with business, he entertained himself and his royal
prisoners—for King David of Scotland shared the
captivity of his brother of France—with the diversion,
best loved in those days by knights and gentlemen, of a
tilting match.   Smithfield, a name associated in our

ears alone with sheep and oxen, was one of the fashionable places for amusement of the sort; and, to give
the greater zest to this particular display of arms, the
king caused it to be published that the Lord Mayor,
the two sheriffs, and the aldermen, would keep the
field against all comers.   Even in those days, when
Lord Mayors and aldermen were much more important
personages than they are now, this announcement produced no little surprise and speculation.   But the fact
was that the king, with his four sons and nineteen of
his nobles, played mayor and corporation on the occasion; and bearing the city arms on their shields and
surcoats, unhorsed or unhelmed, or otherwise damaged
their apparently more aristocratic opponents.   Great
was the delight of the kings, and lords and ladies, who
looked on during these three days' sport.   But greater
still, if possible, was the delight of the good citizens at
the royal and princely condescension thus exhibited in
personating their more plebeian selves.

The termination of the truce, so eagerly looked for,
at length arrived, and King Edward summoned his
barons, and knights, and men of war of all kinds, to
attend him on his new expedition for the subjugation
of France.   So large and well ordered an army never
before left the shores of England.   Such was the
eagerness of all to engage in this fresh attempt to crush
their huge neighbour, that, as an old writer tells us,
" There was not knight, squire, nor man of honour,

from the age of twenty to sixty, that did not go."
There were a hundred thousand of them in all; and,
making the very air ring with shouts of "God and St.
George," they embarked at Sandwich, with Edward the
Black Prince and three of his brothers, on the 27th of
October, 1359. Eleven hundred vessels were required
to carry over this immense force to Calais, where a
miscellaneous gathering of Gascons and Flemings,
under the Duke of Lancaster, awaited them. The duke
had much ado to keep together these needy Gascons
and Flemings; but by dint of giving them money, and
taking them out on little mischief-making and plundering excursions, he preserved their zeal and valour
from evaporating before the much longed-for arrival of
the English army.

The transit to Calais was rapidly performed, the fleet
casting anchor there in the evening of the day on which
it sailed. But the disembarkation was a work of time as
well as of labour, and it was four or five days after its
arrival at Calais before the army was in condition to
begin its march into the country.

That march must have been a sight worth seeing;
full of terrible beauty to those who, like the war-horse
of Scripture, "smelled the battle afar off," and rejoiced
in it!

First came, slow tramping along, five hundred steel-
clad knights, well armed with sword and lance, and the
heavy death-dealing battle-axe. A thousand archers

were in their rear, preceding the king's own battalion, which consisted of three thousand men-at-arms, and five thousand archers.   Immediately behind the king's battalion came the long, long baggage train, extending more than four miles; as we may well believe when we find that it included five thousand waggons, containing not only the usual stores of an army in the enemy's country, rough enough however plentiful, but the added luxuries of handmills to grind their corn, ovens to bake bread, and other things to match.   Formerly they had trusted to chance for a supply of these necessaries. Now, campaigning was beginning to be reduced to a system.   Further, on board these waggons was a number of small boats made of boiled leather, each one large enough to hold three men, and these were to be employed in fishing lakes or streams to provide food during Lent, which in those days was strictly kept as a time of meagre diet.   For diversion by the way, the king had with him a train of thirty falconers with their hawks, and sixty couple of hounds: a royal example that was duly followed by many of his lords and other great men, who also carried with them their hawks and hounds.

The battalion of the prince, with whom rode his three brothers, followed the baggage-train. His was composed of full three thousand men-at-arms, admirably mounted, and glittering in all the military finery of the day. Such surcoats, such scarfs, such tokens from lady-loves! For, in the fourteenth century, it was the fashion to wear scarfs of ribbon, or a knot, or precious glove, purloined from some fair damsel whom the knight professed to admire, and in defence of whose superior beauty he was willing to run a tilt against all comers. Tilting matches of this kind, even between cavaliers of opposing armies, not unfrequently took place to beguile a pause in the fierce encounter of real battle. Five hundred pioneers, with spades and axes to cut down trees and hedges, and level roads, accompanied this array, which marched in such close order as to be ready to engage at a moment's notice, and so watchfully, that not even the meanest lad belonging to the camp was left behind. Woe betide the laggards on that march, for such delayed the whole body, and doubtless would "catch it" for so doing.

The foreign lords were highly gratified by this grand display of military strength, not only because it was admirable in itself, but because having spent all their money, and even some of them pawned their horses and armour while awaiting the king's arrival, the sight of such enormous wealth inspired them with a comfortable hope of his proving a good pay-master, now that he was really come. And they gently intimated as much to the king. Asking for money, however, is always reckoned a terrible test of friendliness, and so it proved on this occasion. The zeal of these lords to serve him (and get plenty of French plunder!) was, of course, very

delightful to the monarch, but—oh, how many fine
things that *but* has spoiled!—he begged to inform
them that in truth he could not afford to pay them for
it; adding graciously that if they chose to remain
with him and share his fortunes, they should receive a
liberal share of the spoil.   For Edward was now fully
bent on either totally subduing France, or inflicting
upon it so severe a chastisement as should enable him
to dictate his own terms of peace.

If a wet blanket had been rudely thrown over all
these noble Gascons and Flemings, they could not have
been more thoroughly dashed and damped than they
were by this royal speech.   Some were so disgusted by
it, that they went straight home, bidding adieu to all
visions of glory and plunder; others were content to
remain, and take their chance of both.

The advance of the army was in a south-easterly
direction, through the old province of Picardy, at that
time a waste desolate country, seeing that for three
years past the ravages of war had stopped all cultiva-
tion of the soil.   Even its wretched inhabitants would
have perished, had not supplies of grain been sent from
more fortunate districts of unfortunate France, so that
of course there was nothing for the invaders to pick up.
Edward had been aware of this beforehand, hence that
ample baggage-train, which was now verily a friend in
need.   Pursuing their route into Champagne, things
somewhat mended; there was more food to be found

on the spot, but as for the weather,—well, it " rained
cats and dogs and swords with their points downwards,"
on these intrusive Englishmen, who were excessively
uncomfortable in consequence.   They might there, had
they been musically disposed, with great appropriate-
ness have sung in chorus their old country song of—

"The rain, it raineth every day."

But spite of wind and weather they fought and plundered their way on to Rheims, the city in which the
kings of France were usually crowned, and where Edward, regarding himself as King of France, had a great
mind to be crowned also.   The city, however, was
strongly held by the French, under one of their arch-
bishops, who was as clever at fighting as at his own
more proper professional duties ; and as before being
crowned within it, it was first needful to take it, Rheims
was invested in due form.

The king took up his quarters at St. Waal, a few
miles from the city; the prince had his at St. Thierry,
and each kept his court in grand style.   A good part
of the winter was spent here, not very pleasantly; for
as Edward was unwilling to risk the storming of so
well fortified a place, little could be done towards pro-
moting his much wished for coronation at Rheims.
The besiegers, however, diverted themselves meanwhile
by making, with various success, occasional forays into
the neighbouring country.

The capture of the garrison of Cormicy was so neatly effected on one of these occasions, that we must stop to relate it. A brave English knight, Sir Bartholomew Burghersh, had his quarters at this place, where the French had so strong and well-defended a castle that they never dreamed of their unpleasant neighbours attacking it. That idea, however, had presented itself to Sir Bartholomew, who examined the fortress thoroughly; and the result of his examination being but to convince him of the hopelessness of taking it by assault, he resolved to try what mining would do for him. To work went his miners with a will, and keeping at it day and night, soon burrowed their way right under the great tower, which they propped up with timber, and then told their lord that they only awaited his signal to throw the whole concern down. Sir Bartholomew, accompanied by his comrade, John de Guistelles, then rode to the castle, and made signs that he wished to have a parley with the governor, Sir Henry de Vaulx. Sir Henry, from the battlements, accordingly bade him say what he wanted. "I want you to surrender," returned the knight, "or you will all be destroyed." On this Sir Henry, who knew nothing about the mine, began to laugh, and asked how it was to be done,—they were perfectly supplied with means of defence, and certainly were not going to surrender simply because the English asked them to do so." "Indeed," said Sir Bartholomew, "if you only knew your situation, you would surrender without more ado." "Why, what *is* our situation," demanded the impatient governor. "Come out, and I will show you," was the reply. On assurance of his safety Sir Henry and three others came out to the two English knights, who immediately conducted them to the mine, and showed them their great tower held up alone by beams of wood.

That sight worked wonders in the Frenchman's mind. With many thanks to the English knight for not miserably destroying them all, as he might have done, he instantly gave up himself and his garrison as prisoners. They were removed from the castle, and after the last had left it, the timber in the mine was set on fire, splitting the tower in two, and bringing the whole down with an awful crash. The governor, who stood with the English looking on, could not, when he saw this fearful spectacle, refrain from again expressing his sense of Sir Bartholomew's noble conduct in saving himself and his people from destruction ; "For," said he, " had our own countrymen of the Jacquerie, who formerly overran this country, had the same advantage over us, they would not have used it so generously."

This was a spirited episode, and a very pleasing one. But as for King Edward and the prince, seven weeks of such stupid work as "sitting down" before Rheims, looking and longing, was quite enough for them ; the more so that their horses were beginning to die off for want of provender. So they gave up the siege of Rheims, and moved on in the same compact vigilant order as before, ravaging and destroying the country, until, on the last day of March, they had advanced within a few miles of Paris.

The aim of the dauphin in defending himself against this alarming invasion had been to avoid coming to any engagement with the enemy, and so to leave him to waste his strength.

This sort of passive resistance, taught him by the disastrous consequences of former pitched battles with those indomitable islanders, did not at all please the English, who, on camping before Paris, sent heralds to invite the dauphin to come forth from behind his protecting gates and walls, and do battle on the open field. The duke, however, was not to be driven from his game; to this invitation he returned a very decided, "No, thank you;" an answer which vexed the king still more. It was as bad as firing at a mud fort, to be always hunting an enemy who would not come out and fight. So, as the dauphin would not come to them, some of the more spirited of the English determined to go to him. The king made a number of new knights, and these together with a few old ones, who were tired of letting their arms rust, set out, under the leadership of Sir Walter de Manny, to attack the barriers of the city. They dashed forward, and had some satisfactory skirmishing between the bars, and so on ; for though there were numbers of French knights who longed to ride out and exchange blows with the English, the dauphin's orders against it were impera- tive, and they were obliged to be content with poking and cutting at each other through the barriers.   Thrust of lance and stroke of sword, however, even under these disadvantages, let out some noble lives; so, as has been said, all were well satisfied.

The last day spent by Edward's immense army, almost beneath the walls of Paris, was signalized by this brisk encounter.   The next morning the king moved away, intending to spend the summer in Brit- tany, and return in the autumn again to try his hand at taking the city of Paris.

The French meanwhile had kept making proposals of peace, to which Edward would not listen, until moved to it by his cousin, the Duke of Lancaster. A violent storm of thunder and lightning, which fright- ened the English nearly out of their wits, backed the duke's arguments effectually.   Edward began to think that heaven itself was offended by his implacable spirit, and at once he avowed his willingness to come to terms.

A treaty was therefore arranged between the two powers on the 8th of May 1360, at Bretigny.   Accord- ing to this, Edward undertook to renounce his claim to the throne of France, in return for several provinces ceded to him, and a ransom of £1,500,000 for the king. This treaty was negotiated by the prince and the dauphin, in the name of the two kings; and, after each had signed it, each, during the time of divine service, ratified it by oath: the dauphin at Paris, the prince at Normandy. Approaching the altar, after these words had been thrice repeated,—"O Lamb of God, that taketh away the sins of the world, grant us thy peace!" —each one laid his right hand upon the consecrated communion bread, and his left upon the holy Gospels, solemnly swearing to observe the treaty. The ceremony ended, the English army was withdrawn from France, leaving, we may presume, few to regret its absence. The king's division was shipped at Calais; he himself joined the prince at Harfleur, where they embarked, and landed at Rye in Sussex on the 18th of May.

All the difficulties in the way of King John's return being thus removed, the prince took him over to Calais in July. The French, however, were not ready with the money part of the agreement at that time, so that it was the 26th of October before the king was really free. Before parting, Edward, who had joined them at Calais, gave a magnificent entertainment to his brother of France. The princes of England and some of the chiefest nobility waited bare-headed on their illustrious guest, and then the two kings graciously bade each other farewell. John took his departure from Calais

on the 28th of the month, the prince, who had courteously entertained him during his delay in that city,
escorting him to Boulogne. Edward himself accompanied his late prisoner for one mile out of Calais;
when anew they parted with apparently friendly feelings in their hearts, hostile as had been their acquaintance.

The prince, on his return to Calais, left France with
his father, and arrived at Dover on the last day of
October. They were welcomed joyfully, for the English were not only very proud of the results of the war,
but, seeing it had cost so much, they were very glad
that it was at an end. The king and prince brought
with them forty hostages for the due fulfilment of the
French treaty, and it was the king's special command
to all his officers that these noblemen should be
courteously treated. A command so faithfully obeyed
that my lords went in and out as they pleased; hunting and hawking when they were so disposed; or,
in quieter mood, making themselves agreeable to the
English ladies.

Our Black Prince, about this period, contrived to
make himself so agreeable to his cousin Joan, called,
on account of her beauty, the Fair Maid of Kent,
that the two were married on the 10th of October
1361.

They were neither of them young—the prince was
thirty-one; and the lady, who was a widow, was a

little older.   The story goes that the prince was pleading the cause of a friend who loved the countess, until
she, tired with his importunities, told him that when
she was young she had been disposed of in marriage
by others, but that now, having come to years of discretion, and being her own mistress, she would please
herself, and certainly would not marry beneath the
royal rank which she inherited from her grandfather
Edward I.

There was something either in what the lady said,
or in her manner of saying it, that at once made the
prince understand that if he asked for himself instead
of his friend, he should not plead in vain.   Upon this
hint he acted, found that his conjecture was quite correct, and they were right royally married at Windsor
Castle.

Christmas was spent at the prince's own manor, or
palace of Berkhampstead in Hertfordshire, about one-
and-twenty miles north-west of London.   This estate
had been given to him and " his heirs for ever " when
he was created Duke of Cornwall; and with its well-
wooded park of more than twelve hundred acres,
abounding with fine fat deer to hunt and to eat, and the
more than princely magnificence with which his household was conducted, it is to be hoped that the prince,
together with the lady his wife, spent their time pleasantly.

The prince's town-house, as we should now call it,

was in the then fashionable neighbourhood of Bil-lingsgate.

King Edward was much pleased with this marriage between his son and the beautiful heiress of Kent, and it proved a happy one.

The Prince's Court in Aquitaine.

EDWARD was well pleased with his bargain of the treaty of Bretigny. But there were others, who had never been taken into the account, who were very much displeased with it. These were the French inhabitants of the provinces ceded to the English, who were grieved to their heart's core when they found they must withdraw their allegiance from their own native sovereign, and yield it to a stranger. Some of them boldly contended that the king had no power thus to transfer them, and they quoted old charters of the Emperor Charlemagne, against this new treaty of King John's. Others, more submissively, wrote pathetic letters to the king, entreating him, "for the love of God," not to do this thing, for they would rather be taxed every year to the half of their property than be turned over to the English. The necessity, however, was too pressing for John to yield either to the solicitations or remonstrances of his distressed people. All he could do was to send soothing messages to them, and remind them that compliance was inevitable, otherwise the treaty would not stand. So they were obliged to give way. " Since our king will have it so," said the people of Rochelle, one of the cities to be given up, " we will do homage to the . English. But our hearts are still French."

One pities these unfortunate Frenchmen. Only think, if we were obliged to swear allegiance to the Emperor of the French ! How ill that would go down. Yet it would not be quite so bad as their case, seeing they were obliged to kiss the hand that had so frequently, since the field of Creçy, smitten them so heavily. We have never endured such degradation from our neighbours.

The governor chosen by Edward for his newly-acquired and newly-confirmed possessions, did honour to his sovereign's choice. Sir John Chandos was the very model of knighthood in the best days of chivalry. " He was," says Froisart, " a most sweet-tempered knight, benign, amiable, courageous, prudent, and sincere in all his dealings." Higher praise could scarcely be bestowed upon man, and we cannot wonder to hear that " none was more beloved and esteemed than he." His establishment as Lord of Aquitaine, Poitou, Guines, and the other ceded provinces in the south, was princely, and he so carried himself as to win the affections of his reluctant subjects. But well as he was liked, the great folks of Aquitaine thought it would be more dignified for them to be governed by the prince in person, who had been recently created Prince of Aquitaine, in addition to being Prince of Wales. At this very juncture also it occurred to the English parliament, busied in finding ways and means for their glorious but costly monarch, that if the prince were to reside on his rich French inheritance, they should have one less of the king's sons to provide for. So, between the two, it fell out that about a couple of years after the cessation of hostilities, our prince was appointed to govern the English possessions in Southern France, in room of the splendid John Chandos.

Great preparations were made for this event; and, after taking leave of the king and queen at the prince's own palace of Berkhampstead, where several days had been passed together, the prince and princess sailed for their new home in February 1363, intending to take up their residence in Bordeaux. A four days' sail landed them "high and dry" at Rochelle, one of the towns that had been so unwilling to be handed over to new masters, and in which this feeling had run so high that for a twelvemonth no Englishman was suffered to enter it. The great Englishman that now presented himself was, however, cordially received. Sir John Chandos, with a stately retinue of nobles and knights, met him there, and four days were spent in festivities. On the fifth, the prince departed for Poitiers, visiting various towns in

the principality before establishing himself in Bordeaux.

His court there was a very magnificent one, at which
the prince received his new subjects most graciously.
Sir John Chandos he made constable of the principality,
and Sir Guiscard d' Angle his marshal. Other English
knights of less note were also placed in office; who, at
a distance, followed their master's example, and kept
up more state than altogether pleased the people of the
country. Perhaps they had a suspicion that they should
have to pay for it !

Sir John Chandos, though after the prince's arrival
he was no longer chief, was yet, next to his master, the
greatest man in the province. An old writer gives an
amusing instance of this. Chandos, with other nobles
and knights, was one day being entertained at court,
when wine was served to the constable immediately
after the prince, and before any one else. The Earl of
Oxford was offended at this; being of higher rank
than Sir John, he thought he ought to have been served
before him; so, when Chandos' squire brought him
the cup, he angrily bade the young man give it to his
master. The squire, who possibly had as good blood
in his veins as my lord of Oxford, was quite equal to
this emergency. "Why should I do that," said he
fiercely, "seeing he has already drunk ? Drink yourself, since it is offered you, for, by St. George, if you
do not, I will throw it in your face !" In very fear

that this bold squire would do as he threatened, the earl drank, or pretended to drink, and there the matter ended for the time. But, when the prince had retired, Sir John, who had noticed what passed, came up and administered a quiet but most stinging rebuke to the presumptuous earl. "What," said he, "are you displeased that I drank first, who am constable of this country! I may well take precedence of you, seeing my sovereign chooses to have it so. It is true you were at the battle of Poitiers, but since the lords present know not how that came to pass I shall tell them, that it may not be forgotten. You came back from France without leave, contrary to the king's commands, who, when he saw you, ordered you instantly to return thither to your duty under pain of forfeiting life and lands. And that is how you came to be at the battle, where you commanded only forty lances, while I had sixty. Bethink you then whether I do not well to take precedence of, and drink before you."

The poor foolish earl was so confounded by this terrible setting down, that he had not a word to say, and as our historian relates, wished himself anywhere but where he was.

There was still great difficulty in getting the French treaty properly executed. The Duke of Anjou, son of King John, had been one of the hostages given to King Edward for its due performance; and this young prince disgracefully broke his parole, or word of hon-

our not to escape. He had obtained permission to be
removed from London to Calais, pretending that his
being there would facilitate the settlement of affairs;
but once in Calais, he was soon off home again. King
John was deeply offended by this act of his son's, and
determined on returning to England himself, partly to
excuse his son, partly in the hope that he and King
Edward together might make provision for ending
these troubles. His counsellors were strongly opposed
to such a measure. They did not care whether the
treaty were scrupulously fulfilled on their part or not,
and, in plain terms, they told him that he would be
very foolish if he again put himself in the power of
the English king. But John's high sense of honour
could not brook that any fault should rest upon him;
and telling his counsellors that though good faith
were banished from the rest of the world, it should
still be found in the breast of kings, he took ship, and
arrived in London about Christmas 1363. He was
received with all honour, as such a man deserved.
Indeed, there appeared to exist a very cordial feeling
between King Edward and himself. Edward, who was
with his queen at his fine palace of Eltham, sent a
retinue of knights to Dover to welcome his royal
visitor and bring him to the palace, where he arrived
on the Sunday afternoon. They did not keep Sunday
in those days as we do now; for we are told they
entertained themselves with singing and dancing, in

which one of the young French lords particularly distinguished himself, until supper-time.

On entering London, the citizens came out with much reverence to meet John, and bring him to his former residence of the Savoy. There, throughout the winter, the royal family visited him in the most friendly manner; and there, unhappily, this chivalrous monarch, being seized with illness, breathed his last, in about a year after his leaving France: sincerely mourned by king, queen, and the princes of England. His son, the Dauphin Charles, succeeded to his crown. The body of John was embalmed, carried to France, and there solemnly interred in the cathedral of St. Denis. The ceremony ended with a magnificent dinner!

The Prince led a stately and quiet life in his principality of Aquitaine. Here, attracted by his fame, came Peter, king of Cyprus and Jerusalem, to see with his own eyes the hero with whose praises all the civilized world rang. Peter, who had done battle valiantly against the Turks in Palestine, had been making a roving sort of tour through Europe, for the purpose of urging its various monarchs to assume the Red Cross, and join him in a fresh crusade in the East. He was well received by all, and had promises from some—fine speeches from others. By the King of England and his queen he was welcomed with uncommon magnificence. Such dinners, such suppers, such entertainments were provided in his honour! But as for going on crusade, Edward said he was too old for that,—too discreet, he very likely meant; though he readily granted permission to such of his knights as desired it, to go to Peter's assistance. The King of Cyprus would also fain have had the Prince's help for his crusade. Till he had seen him, he said, he had done little; so he crossed over, and the Prince, who then kept his court at Angoulême, hearing of his arrival at Poitiers, sent Chandos, with a handsome retinue, to meet and bring His Majesty of Cyprus to him. The king was just in time for a grand tournament, held in celebration of the birth of the Prince's eldest son, Edward, and altogether was treated with great distinction; but the Prince, like his father, declined going a-crusading with him. Still Peter was delighted with his host; delighted also to find that, though he could not prevail on the Prince to take up arms with him, he was free to enlist for this holy war as many of the English and Gascon knights in the province as he liked.

But though the Prince refused to measure his strength against infidels in the East, quiet and he were not long to be acquainted. It suited neither mind nor body. Work of his own sort was presently found him, and it came about in this way:— During King Edward's long wars in France, vast numbers of mere soldiers of fortune had banded themselves together—men who would fight for either party that would pay them best.   A rascally sort of thing; but it must be owned that there were some fine fellows amongst them, especially among their leaders, who were chiefly English and Gascons.   The peace of Bretigny might have thrown these men out of employment, but that the King of Navarre—him whom John had suspected of giving bad advice to the dauphin—quarrelled with his old friend Charles after the latter came to the throne, and a teazing little warfare was kept up between them, which found employment in the fighting line for those who wanted it; while at the same time there was the old chronic contest going on, to decide whether the Lord Charles of Blois, whom the French had always backed, or the Earl of Montfort, for whom the English as pertinaciously stood up, should have the duchy of Brittany.   But Navarre and France at last patched up their quarrel.   The aunt and sister of the former king had the merit of bringing this about.   And as it had been settled, by hard blows, that the Earl of Montfort should henceforth be Duke of Brittany, the difficulty then was to know how to dispose of the tools with which this stern handicraft of fighting had been carried on; for these soldiers of fortune, or Free Companions, as they called themselves, finding their occupation gone, became a terror to the inhabitants, whom they pillaged and plundered without mercy.   Their old marauding habits so clung to them that they could not throw them off.   Indeed, they said that France was their own domain, and they *would* live by pillage. The Pope was good enough to excommunicate them, but they did not care a fig for that; and as there were nearly fifty thousand of them scouring the country, seizing towns and castles, and thence laying the neighbourhood under contribution, the evil was a serious one, that exceedingly puzzled French statesmen to remedy. The King of England had covenanted with the King of France to assist him in putting down these pillagers, who resolutely refused to disband when bidden to do so; but Edward, in his zeal, got ready so large a force for this purpose, that Charles, in a fright, hastened to decline his help. He had no notion of letting so many fighting Englishmen enter his dominions, whatever might be the pretext; so he undertook to get rid of them himself.

Fortunately for him, in 1366 an opportunity occurred of finding occupation in Spain for these unquiet spirits and restless bodies. Pedro, king of Castile, called the Cruel, (a name that he well deserved,) had for his misdeeds been deposed, and his kingdom bestowed upon Don Henry, who was called his brother. But not being himself disposed to acquiesce in this transfer of his property, he took up arms to defend his rights. Henry did the same to maintain his claim, and the French determined to aid the latter by sending him a great batch of these insupportable Free Companions. For money they would have gone to fight in the moon, had there been any way of getting there; so they made no difficulty about crossing the Pyrenees. It cost a good deal to send them out, but it was indeed building a bridge of gold for a retreating enemy, which is always reckoned good policy; and the French did not grudge the price. The only stipulation made by the Companions was, that they should not be employed against the Prince of Wales in Aquitaine. Some of them had served under his banner, and his chivalrous character must deeply have impressed even these hirelings, seeing that though they were ready enough to take service with another, they were unwilling to bear arms against one so good and so great as our Prince.

Sir Bertrand du Guesclin, one of the greatest warriors that France ever produced, led the Companions into Spain. He took them by way of Avignon, where the Pope was, and demanded, first, that his fellows should be released from the excommunication pronounced against them; secondly, that the Pope should furnish him with a large sum of money. There was no difficulty about granting the first request; the second was altogether a different affair. But as Du Guesclin assured the Pope that the second was much the more important of the two—absolution they could do without, but money was indispensable—he was obliged to give them both. So they went on their way rejoicing; their prowess (for they *could* fight) soon confirming Don Henry on his throne, and driving Don Pedro out of the country.

Pedro, however, was not going to take the matter quietly. The fame of the Prince of Wales had spread far and wide—fame, not only for valour and military genius, but for his other knightly qualities of generosity and goodness. So this horrible Pedro, who was an utter wretch, finding himself deprived of his kingdom, wrote a piteous letter, recounting his misfortunes to the Prince, and praying him, "for the love of God," to help him in the recovery of his dominions, from which the Pope, his own brother, and the Free Companions had driven him.

The humane and generous temper of the Prince was touched by this appeal. Perhaps we may also believe that his military ardour was roused by the prospect of fresh fields to be fought and won; for with him fighting and winning had ever been one. But he was too prudent a man to do anything hastily. King Pedro's letter and supplications were placed before two of the prince's counsellors, and these two wise heads, having laid themselves together, came to the conclusion that the prince would do well to grant Pedro's request, and march forthwith into Spain for his help. Others of his counsellors, equally wise and wary, were, however, of a different mind; and thus they advised their prince:—"My Lord, it is true that you are one of the most notable princes in the world, and are, God be

(3)   11

thanked! at peace with every one. It is also well
known that, for repute of your knighthood, no king
dare anger you. You ought, therefore, to be content
with what you have, and not seek for enemies. This
Don Pedro is a man cruel, proud, and ill-disposed,
who has done so much evil in his kingdom that therefore his people have driven him away. He has done
grievous wrong to his neighbours, and, moreover, it is
commonly said that he murdered the young lady his
wife, your cousin, daughter of the Duke of Bourbon.
It were therefore well to bethink you before you succour him; for what he now endures are chastisements
from God, who orders them that kings and princes
of this world may therefore learn not to commit like
wickednesses."

The prince was not particularly pleased with this,
and, in reply, told his lords that he was perfectly
acquainted with all Don Pedro's ill deeds; but still,
spite of them, it was neither decent nor proper that
one who was not really his brother, though called so,
should take his crown from him; and no king's son
ought to suffer it. Further, his father and King Pedro
had been allies, and that was another reason why he
should render the aid requested of him.

His lords were still of the same mind,—that he should
stay at home, and leave King Pedro and King Henry
to fight it out between themselves. But not a bit
could they prevail with the prince, who every day be-

came more eager to set out on this expedition to
Spain.   King Pedro, meanwhile, had followed his
letter, bringing his three daughters with him; and,
hearing of his arrival, the prince rode out from Bordeaux to meet him, escorting him to that city with
all honour and courtesy; for, in addition to his military renown, the prince had that of being the best-
bred gentleman of his time.   In conversation, Pedro
backed his request by so many promises of what he
would do in return, as were enough to tempt any
ambitious man.   The prince's son was to be made
king of Gallicia, in Spain; while such unheard-of
riches were to be showered, both upon the prince and
his followers, as set both English and Gascons a-long-
ing to go and do battle for this same Pedro.

In an evil hour the prince had his own way, and
began to make preparations for carrying an army into
Spain.   About twelve thousand of the most noted
Free Companions were invited to join his standard,
and even those who had served in Spain against Don
Pedro gladly prepared to change sides and fight for
him.   Over and above his own followers, four hundred English men-at-arms and archers joined the
prince, under his brother the Duke of Lancaster.
Flemings and Germans he might have had in plenty,
had he cared for them; but he did not wish to have
strangers about him.   Money, the sinews of war, had
also to be provided in large quantity; for the prince

had undertaken to pay the cost of the expedition, on faith of Pedro's promise to re-imburse him. A portion of the late French king's ransom became due at this time, quite opportunely, and to swell the amount the prince, by the advice of Chandos and Sir William Felton, melted down and coined his gold and silver plate. It was a pity to take such pains and expense for so hopeless a villain as Don Pedro.

Securing men, money, and other munitions of war consumed much time; so that it was the 10th of January 1367 before the prince left Bordeaux on his way to fight Don Pedro's quarrels. His second son, Richard, afterwards king of England, was born only a few days before the prince entered upon this Spanish expedition.

One of the fine promises by which Pedro tempted the prince to his aid, and which he thought important enough to be confirmed by a legal document, makes one smile. It was, that if at any time the King of England, the prince, and their successors, kings or princes of England, should have a fancy for fighting, under the banner of His Majesty of Castile, against the infidels—that is, Turks or Moors—the said king and his three eldest sons should have the chief command of the vanguard—the post of honour—in preference to any other princes of Christendom. And in case they did not feel disposed to avail themselves of this gracious permission to serve under him, the English standard should be set up in the same place, by way of asserting their pre-eminent dignity in the army !

But in those days the Turks were a *power* in Europe, not a name only; the Moors held large possessions in Spain; and as Mohammedans they were reckoned the common enemies of Christendom.

The Prince's Spanish Campaign.

BEFORE setting out for Spain, the prince had bargained with the King of Navarre for a free passage through his dominions. But as the army slowly advanced on its route, such alarming reports of the king's bad faith (which his past character led them to believe) were made to its commanders as induced some of them to bring things to a point by attacking him. Sir Hugh Calverly, a distinguished leader of the Free Companions, pressed forward and took two towns belonging to Navarre, and this brought the king himself, in a rage, to confer with the prince. The result of their conference was, that the previous stipulation of a free passage was confirmed; and that fine army of thirty thousand men, under the most renowned commander of the age, began streaming through the various defiles in the Pyrenees, which give France access to Spain.

Passing the Pyrenees, however, in the winter season is no trifling matter, especially for armies, with their cumbrous baggage waggons. It is true there was no enemy to oppose them,—in those mountain passes a handful of men might have kept a whole army at bay, —but there were natural difficulties to contend with, and to meet these, so far as was possible, the entire force was divided into three bodies, one of which was to march through them each day. The vanguard, amounting to twelve thousand cavalry, passed on the Monday. It was commanded by the Duke of Lancaster, with whom was the brave Chandos, at the head of his own company of twelve hundred lances, all bearing the knight's arms on their pennons. On Tuesday the prince's division of ten thousand horse scrambled through, with bitter wind and snow in their teeth chilling them to the very bones. With him was Don Pedro, together with the King of Navarre, who, in the excess of his complaisance, was now doing the honours of his own country to the prince. They halted at Pampeluna, where the king treated his travel-worn friends to a good supper. Wednesday saw the remainder of the army safe through the defile, and then the whole camped for several days' rest in the valley of Pampeluna, where food for man and horse was abundant.

In this land of plenty the Free Companions, falling into their old habits, made themselves rather more free than welcome. It had been arranged between the king and prince that provision for the army should be found on payment for it; but these rovers very much preferred *snatching* it to acquiring it in so tame a manner as by purchase. Pillaging came so naturally to them that, in truth, they *could* not refrain; and the King of Navarre was not a little vexed with himself for permitting such vagabonds free entrance into his country. However, there they were, and all that he could do was to entreat them to be a little better behaved, which they graciously promised.

On marching further into the country the advanced guard of the prince's army came in contact with some of King Henry's troops, and a little skirmishing took place between the two. Henry himself sent his antagonist a formal challenge to battle, and his boldness rather pleased the prince than otherwise. "He must be a valiant gentleman," said he, "to write me such a letter;" and awaiting an attack from him, the army was drawn up in order of battle, with banners and pennons waving, at Vittoria, where, near five centuries later, another English hero was to gather one of his many laurels. During this pause the honour of knighthood was conferred on many of the prince's followers. Among those advanced to this dignity were his own step-son, Sir Thomas Holland (the fair Joan, it will be remembered, was a widow when the prince married her) and the worthless Don Pedro; three hundred new made knights in all were that day waiting, with all the impatience imaginable, to show that they had deserved their spurs.

They waited in vain, however. King Henry, hourly expecting reinforcements, both from Arragon and under Du Guesclin,—the latter was bringing him four thousand men,—hung fire till it was too late to do anything. And though the prince was quite in a mood to fight had the chance been offered him, yet he was not displeased that the day passed over quietly, as his rear division of more than six thousand men had not yet come up. When night fell his people all returned to their quarters, the order being, that when the trumpet sounded next morning, they were to form in the same order as before. The enemy, however, was beforehand with them! At peep of dawn next day six thousand well mounted, well armed Spaniards, under the king's brothers Dons Tello and Sancho, rode forth to make an early visit to the English camp. As the sun rose on their long glittering files, they fell in with a body of Companions belonging to Sir Hugh Calverly, which they attacked and defeated, carrying off their baggage, and forcing Sir Hugh to fly post haste to the Duke of Lancaster's division, whose vanguard was next set upon by the victorious Spaniards, with loud shouts of " Castile," " Castile." The attack was so sudden and impetuous that down went tents, huts, and everything before it, and the whole division was drawn out to meet the enemy as hastily as the disorder into which it was thrown would permit, the rest of the army getting into motion after it. The Spaniards, who had no

notion of fighting so many, retreated in good order
when they saw the extensive preparations for receiving
them, but meeting on their way an advanced guard of
about two hundred English and Gascons, under Sir
William Felton, they ventured to charge them. Six
thousand against two hundred left no doubt as to the
result, though it cost the swarming Spaniards some
hours' hard fighting before the last of that valorous
little company was slain. Their leader, Sir William, was
among the first, for, after having drawn up his troop on
a slight eminence, he dashed, lance in rest, full gallop
into the midst of the enemy, running one of their
knights right through the body, armour and all, and
then flinging him dead out of the saddle. The Spaniards instantly closed round the gallant Englishman,
but though his strong arm dealt around such blows as
that few required a second stroke, he was overpowered
and at last killed. A few boys alone escaped, by the
swiftness of their horses, to carry this disastrous news
to their prince.

King Henry was exceedingly delighted when his returning troops narrated to him the brisk doings of the
day; and in the joy of his heart, he received their success as an omen of the easy and entire destruction of
the English army. An old French commander, however, who was present and knew better, stopped the
king, assuring him that when he came to meet the
prince in person, he would then find "tough and hardy"

knights, men who would die where they stood soonei
than think of flying. He therefore entreated him not
to risk a battle with the prince, but rather starve him
out by guarding all the passes and defiles so strictly
that no provision could reach him; in which case he
would soon be obliged to take himself off home again.

But the king was not to be persuaded. He thought
of his overpowering numbers,—a hundred thousand
well armed and determined men,—and of the glory of
beating (as he intended doing) so renowned a commander as the Prince of Wales, and he took his resolution accordingly. " By the soul of my father," said
he, " I have such a desire to see this prince, and try
my strength with him, that we will never part without
a battle." And so the old Frenchman was silenced.

After some marching and manœuvring, amid wind,
rain, and snow, and such scarcity of provision in the
prince's camp that a small loaf was sold for a florin,
the two armies came in sight of each other between
Navarretta and Najara, in Old Castile, on the 2d of
April 1367, and each was drawn up in order to be
ready for battle on the morrow.

The bright armour of these glittering battalions was
a beautiful sight when the sun rose upon them next
day. The prince, with some of his officers, ascended a
rising ground, and seeing the enemy marching upon
them, formed his own line in the plain, and then halted.
The Spaniards, perceiving what he was about, did the

same, and then each man tightened his armour for the combat.

While they thus stood facing each other, Sir John Chandos advanced in front of the English, with his banner in his hand; for, after the manner of those times, in presence of the enemy he was to have the rank of a knight-banneret conferred upon him. This was a very high dignity, since he who received it must not only be a valiant soldier, and ordinarily a gentleman by birth, but was also required to have such an extent of landed property as to have gentlemen by birth for his vassals, who, in time of war, ranged themselves under his banner. John Chandos was both a valiant soldier and of gentle birth, and he could bring into the field knights enough to meet the third qualification. The ceremony was performed in this manner:—Presenting his banner to the prince, "My lord," said he, "here is my banner, which I offer you that I may display it in such manner as may best please you; for I have sufficient lands to enable me to do so, and maintain the rank which it ought to hold." The prince, taking the banner, cut off the point to make it square, —for in those days a square banner was a peg higher in dignity than a pointed or swallow-tailed one,—and then returned it to its owner, saying,—" Sir John, I return your banner; God grant you strength and honour to preserve it."

The newly docked banner was received with acclamation when Sir John went back with it to his company. Every man among them felt that he was a step higher in the world than before, and vowed that, with God's help, he would worthily defend it. A vow that, before sunset, was as worthily performed.

The two armies now began to move towards each other, but before they met, the prince, raising his eyes and hands towards heaven, uttered aloud this devout prayer:—" God of truth, the Father of Jesus Christ, Who hast made and fashioned me, grant through Thy grace that the success of this battle may be for me and my army; for Thou knowest that in truth I have been solely emboldened to undertake it in the support of justice and reason, to reinstate this king on his throne, who has been disinherited and driven from it, as well as from his country." And with that, taking Don Pedro by the hand,—" Sir King," said he, " you shall this day know whether you have anything in the kingdom of Castile or not." Then crying out,—" Advance banners in the name of God and St. George," the two armies came clashing together in mortal combat.

The battalion of Lancaster and Chandos first engaged with that under du Guesclin, and the old French marshal who had advised starvation instead of fighting; and a tough fight those veterans made of it. Neither would give way, and they got terribly mixed up together, in the struggle each to force back the other. The prince's division charged another body of Spaniards, one of whose leaders (he who, with his thousands, had at last destroyed those poor two hundred English and Gascons) took fright, and rode straight off the field with two thousand of his horsemen. The remainder were soon disposed of, and then the prince fell upon the division commanded by King Henry himself, in which there was at least forty thousand horse and foot. Here the battle began in good earnest. In addition to sword, lance, and axe, some of these troops were armed with slings, from which they hurled stones with so much violence as to break through the steel helmets of their adversaries. English arrows came deadlily among them in return, and the plain resounded with cries of,— "Castile for King Henry," "St. George for Guienne."

Sir John Chandos did honour to his new banner; but pressing forward too eagerly, he was surrounded, unhorsed, and would have been slain by a huge Castilian, who bore him to the ground, but for a knife that he carried in his bosom, with which, as he lay under his antagonist, he stabbed him to death in the back and sides, and then threw him off. He afterwards rejoined his own people, who had made their way to the spot where he had fallen; and the capture, among others, of the celebrated du Guesclin, was the splendid trophy of the new banneret's arms.

The English and Gascons fought bravely, and so did some of the Spaniards; but panic possessed so many of them that it was in vain for King Henry to rally his troops. Thrice he checked their flight, and brought them again to the charge, but it was in vain; the prince, with his thirty thousand, was more than a match for the Spanish king's hundred thousand, who fled in all directions; Don Henry himself at last mounting his horse, and galloping off with the runaways. They were closely pursued as far as Najara, which the English entered pell-mell with them; and in that headlong chase numbers fell, slain by the enemy, or drowned in the river, into which they leaped in hope of escape from the murderous weapons behind, and whose current was tinged with the blood of men and horses. This town of Najara yielded a rich spoil to the first comers, in the shape of plate and jewels belonging to Don Henry and his nobles.

The defeat, which was accomplished before noon of that April morning was total and deadly; and as the enemy was swept away, the prince fixed his banner upon a bush hard by as a rallying point for his men, who gradually drew up around him in fine order, even after so hardly fought a battle.

Pedro, hot from the pursuit, galloped up on a black courser, but seeing the prince, dismounted, approached him on foot, and would have kneeled while he thanked his deliverer, had not the prince prevented him. Taking the king by the hand,—" Cousin," said he, " give thanks to God, for to Him belongs the praise; the victory comes from Him, and not from me."

A monarch, one who, for his genius, his grandeur, and the strange vicissitudes of his life, was one of the most remarkable that ever reigned, said between three and four thousand years ago,—" The help that is done upon earth God doeth it Himself!" Edward, Prince of Wales and Acquitaine, the victor of three well fought fields, *knew* this, and had the moral courage to avow it to that reprobate Don Pedro.

The ample provision of King Henry's camp, all of which he left behind him in his flight, furnished a welcome refreshment for the prince's hungry army. It was not the first time that his troops had been indebted to the vanquished for a meal; nor need we wonder at being told that they enjoyed their supper. Under King Henry's deserted tents they made themselves comfortable for the night, and spent the next day, which was Palm Sunday, in needful rest. By six o'clock on that morning the prince was up and receiving such of his officers as waited upon him. Among them came King Pedro, who was most graciously welcomed, but who more than startled his princely host by courteously requesting that the prisoners should be given up to him that he might cut their heads off! This was rather too much. The prince paused a moment, and then told the king that *he* also had a request to make, which he entreated, for the sake of their friendliness, might not be refused. The king, who could deny nothing to the man who had just restored his crown to him, cheerfully promised to grant it whatever it might be. So the prince made his request, which was that Pedro should pardon all his rebellious subjects, with the exception of one flagrant offender, with whom he might do as he pleased.

It was very disappointing to Pedro the Cruel not to be allowed to cut off so many heads when they were in his power. But as he was obliged to comply with the prince's wish, he swallowed his vexation, and, like sensible man, did what was required of him as though he liked doing it. Nay, more, when the prince deli vered up the prisoners to him, he kissed his brother Don Sancho, who was one of them (Don Henry and Don Tello were neither of them there to be kissed), and to all save the excepted one (who was instantly beheaded outside the tent), promised forgiveness of the past if they would only do better in future. The prince's humanity that day saved many lives; nor did he forget to show kindly courtesies to the Spanish nobles who had been his captives.

Don Pedro with his suite then rode off to Burgos, the capital of Old Castile, leaving the prince and his army still in camp. Next day after evening prayers, the camp was broken up, and he marched after the king to Burgos, which he entered in state, with his brother the Duke of Lancaster and other nobles. His army lay in the surrounding plains, the prince being entertained in the city; though his tent was pitched in the midst of his brave fellows whom he visited every day.

News of this, the prince's third great victory, speedily passed into France, England, Germany, and other European countries, where it added vastly to his renown. Some of his enthusiastic admirers declared that such a prince as he, was worthy of governing the whole world. By his countrymen this astounding feat of arms of settling a disputed succession by one blow, was celebrated with much feasting and pageantry. But in France there was mourning and lamentation, for their many warriors fallen in the battle, and for their greatest of all, du Guesclin, who was an unransomed prisoner.

Rather more than three weeks were spent at Burgos, and then, seeing that the rebellion was crushed, and Pedro secure on his throne, by the renewed allegiance of his subjects, the prince thought proper to put him in mind of their agreement, before setting out from Aquitaine. So he begged that the money which he had advanced for the expedition might be repaid him as speedily as possible, that they might get them gone, otherwise he feared his men-at-arms might begin to help themselves. The king assured him that he would faithfully fulfil all that he had promised, but, unfortunately, at that moment, he had no money. He would go immediately to Seville, and there procure enough to satisfy the prince's army, which he recommended should be meanwhile marched into the fertile country about Valladolid, where, by Whitsuntide at latest, he would himself join them, with the needful funds.

This sounded so fair that the prince and his council were content. Off set Pedro in one direction seeking money, and off set the prince in another, to find good quarters for his men.

The English kept wearily waiting at Valladolid, the Companions beguiling their tedium by a little pillaging, according to their wont; but no Pedro made his appearance, neither did he think it worth while to send word why he did not come. Perplexed and annoyed at this, the prince, by the advice of his council, despatched three knights to the city of Sevile, (almost at the other side of the country, and where Pedro was all the time,) to demand the reason of this non-fulfilment of his promise. The king pretended to be exceedingly delighted to see these knights, and he told them politely how very sorry he was that he had been unable to do as he promised his good friend the prince. He had himself remonstrated with his subjects, and set others to do the same, on their slowness in bringing in supplies, but his people excused themselves by saying it was impossible to collect any money so long as the Free Companions were in the country. These vagabonds had, as he declared, already killed three or four of his officers, who were actually on their way to the prince with money; and he therefore begged that the prince might be entreated, from him, to be good enough to send those wicked Companions right away home, and leave some of his knights, to whom the amount due should be scrupulously paid. And with this he bade the prince's messengers farewell.

They returned to their master with the answer they had got; and its delivery perplexed and annoyed him still more, for he now began to suspect that Pedro meant to shuffle out of his engagements. The cunning Castilian had, according to the French proverb, sucked the orange, and was now preparing to throw away the rind. The prince was deeply wounded; to a man of his high sense of honour such shabbiness was inexpressibly offensive, and he had the further mortification of reflecting that it was for such a one that he had so freely poured out blood and treasure, and thrown away his own strength in that destructive climate. For the four months that he had spent about Valladolid, were the four hottest months of that hot portion of the Continent; and prince and people were alike all wasting under it. The army was in haste to leave so unhealthy a country; indeed, it appears that in those days the English had a great dislike to the climate of Spain. Castile, they complained, was full of barren rocks and mountains, the rivers were angry, brawling streams, and its inhabitants were beggarly. While as for Spanish wines, of which we, in our day, make so much

account, the being obliged to drink them was another
of the grievances attending service in Spain.   They
said these wines were so strong and fiery, that they
disordered their heads, and consumed their lungs and
liver; so that, between hot suns and hot wines,
Englishmen, "who in their own country were sweetly
nourished" with good meat and ale, and who made a
tolerable shift to live in the pleasant country of France,
were in Castile, "burnt within and without."   "Rough-
ing it" on a bottle of port with their beef-steak, was
evidently opposed to the notions of these grumbling
Englishmen.   Then the nights were so overpoweringly
hot, that they could not bear any bed-clothes, while the
extreme cold of early morning came on so suddenly,
that all unclothed as they were, it threw them into
fevers and other maladies.   Altogether Spain was not
to their mind; especially now that the ungrateful Pedro
was going to leave them to their own resources, spite
of his solemn engagements to the contrary.   There was
another reason why they should get back again as quickly
as possible.   King Henry when he fled, had hastened
into France, where, by the connivance of the Duke of
Anjou, he was now threatening Aquitaine, of which the
Princess of Wales, in the absence of her lord, had been
left guardian.   And though the French king with
whom the English were at peace, had peremptorily forbidden Henry's attacking the prince's dominions, it yet
was time for him to be at home and take care of himself

Orders were therefore issued for the immediate return of the army. The King of Majorca, who had been a brave comrade of the brave prince, was too ill in bed to be removed when they departed, so they were obliged to leave him behind. The prince would fain have had some of his people stay to protect his friend, but even that, the self-denying monarch refused, for he said he knew not how long he might be confined there by illness. So tents were struck, baggage-waggons piled, and those whom war and climate had spared, began their march homewards; conquerors, yet sufferers.

There had been difficulties in getting into Spain. There were now difficulties in getting out of it, for some of the mountain-passes on the borders of Arragon were closed against them; by the evil influence of that bad King of Navarre, as it was said; and this caused a whole month's detention of the army, on its route, while negotiations were carried on with the King of Arragon, for passage through his share of the Pyrenees. In truth it was not the fault of the King of Navarre that these passes were not open; but he was so very bad and untrustworthy a character, that if anything went wrong where he was at all concerned, people took for granted that it was his doing. He made his appearance, however, as soon as the King of Arragon had consented to let his kingdom be turned into a thoroughfare for a while, waited respectfully upon the prince, and by way of not being outdone in courtesy by his brother of Arragon, offered a free passage through his own kingdom of Navarre, (which was a much shorter route than that through Arragon) to the prince, the Duke of Lancaster, and some other knights. The rest of the army might, for him, get home as they liked, and when they liked. The prince gladly accepted this offer for himself and his friends; and such was his influence with the king that he finally induced him to extend his permission to the entire army.

They marched as quietly as possible through Navarre, for that was in the covenant, and the king himself attended them to the borders of his kingdom; partly, it may be supposed, to do honour to the most notable prince in Europe, partly, no doubt, to see that their engagements to keep the peace and pay honestly for such things as they required, should be respected by the English and Gascons under his command. At Bayonne, the frontier town of his own possessions, the prince halted to give a few days' rest to his weary and weakened frame; for this expedition to Spain had given him his death-blow; and then he pursued his route to Bordeaux. His reception there was stately, befitting the return of a victorious monarch. But it was loving also; for the wife who had been so sad at thought of his going away, came out to meet him, bringing with her his little son Edward, then a child of three years old.

XII

Troubles in Aquitaine.

THIS Spanish expedition brought great glory to the prince; and that was all. The injury it did him was incalculable. His health was utterly broken; some supposed that slow poison had been secretly administered to him by his enemies; but his illness was more probably the result of climate and. hardships. And thanks to the worthless Pedro, he brought back with him from Spain a load of debt that, as we shall presently see, ultimately led to the destruction of English power in southern France. That was a heavy price to pay for the world's plaudits.

The prince's first care on reaching home, was to disperse the remains of his army. The great men of it took care of themselves; the Gascon lords with their retainers returned to their own castles, the English knights to their various offices in the province; and those from over seas followed their leader, the Duke of Lancaster, to England. But the Free Companies still remained to be disposed of. They would not disperse until they had received their pay; and as Don Pedro's promise to pay had been found worse than valueless, the prince was obliged to pledge himself to them for payment, and meanwhile suffer them to make themselves at home in Aquitaine. For he said, that though Don Pedro had broken faith with him, it would ill become him to act in like manner towards those who had served him so well. These dangerous visitors were therefore to remain where they were until he could raise money enough to satisfy their demands. This was no easy matter; the Spanish expedition had completely impoverished the prince, and as the Companions, amounting to six thousand men, presently began to meet the difficulty by living at free quarters upon the indignant inhabitants, he had no resource but to beg them to take themselves out of his dominions, as for the present he could do nothing for them.

Strange to say, these rude, unprincipled men did as they were requested. They had no objection to living by plunder, nay, as has been said, they liked it; but for his very valiancy and goodness, they preferred *not* to plunder their old master, provided they could be equally well served elsewhere. And as France, their "own domain" was open to them, they trooped thither, to the great satisfaction of the prince's subjects, and the extreme dismay of those of King Charles. So this danger was staved off for awhile.

The prince's Spanish and French prisoners had been

duly ransomed, and had gone home, with the exception
of the brave du Guesclin, who still remained in bondage.
He was thought so essential to the defeated King
Henry, that the prince's advisers were unwilling to let
him go, before Don Pedro had paid his long bill, for
fear of another Spanish contest, in which, with no
Prince of Wales to contend against, the Frenchman
and his master would certainly have the best of it.
So he was left to chafe and fret, and get on as he best
could in this enforced idleness.

During his captivity, the prince one day, good
humouredly, asked du Guesclin how he was. "Never,
better, my lord," was the answer, "I cannot be otherwise than well, seeing I am the most honoured knight
in the world." The prince did not exactly see that,
and bade him explain himself. In reply he was told
that throughout France and Spain, it was said that the
reason why du Guesclin was left a prisoner was that
the prince was so afraid of him, that he _dared_ not set
him at liberty. And that, the knight ventured to
think, was paying him a very high compliment. The
prince could not stand this. It might be a joke, or it
might be earnest; but not for one moment could he
endure the idea of anybody's thinking that he feared
living man. "By St. George," was his prompt rejoinder, "it is not so." And he told the knight, that
on payment of a ransom, amounting to about ten
thousand pounds, he should immediately be free. It

is supposed that the prince thought du Guesclin could not command so large an amount, and therefore that he should hear no more about his ransom. But he was mistaken. Du Guesclin, who knew his own value, and how his countrymen rated him, snapped at the offer, thanking the prince for putting so high a price upon him; a price which he declared would be raised if every old woman in France had to contribute the produce of her spinning-wheel towards it.

The prince's counsellors blamed him very much for suffering himself to be thus trapped into liberating the most formidable of his opponents, before Don Pedro's coin was forthcoming; and they advised him to break his word with the prisoner. But though vexed enough at himself the prince could not do that. He had "promised," certainly to "his hurt," but "changing," on that account, was a thing not to be thought of. Du Guesclin was accordingly liberated on his parole, and, by the help of the King of France and the Duke of Anjou, within one month paid the large sum demanded of him. As had been feared, the knight immediately returned to the aid of Don Henry; who taking up arms a second time against the detested Pedro, overthrew, and murdered him with his own hand.

The worn-out frame of the prince required rest, now that he was at home. But instead of rest he was plunged into cares and vexations. The death of Pedro put an end to all chance of payment of his large debt,

if indeed there had been any chance before.   And as
the prince considered himself responsible, to those who
had fought under him, for the satisfaction of their just
claims, it was incumbent upon him to provide money
in one way or other.   Pedro might defraud him, but
it was impossible for him to defraud others.   The only
way in which it appeared to him that he could raise
the requisite funds, was by imposing a heavy tax upon
his subjects.   This tax was called the Fouage; it was
literally a tax upon every chimney or house-fire in the
province; and it excited the liveliest discontent among
the inhabitants of the whole principality.   A parliament
was summoned at Niort, to whom the prince's chancellor
announced the impost, explaining how it was to be
levied, and that it was not designed to last more than
five years, or at any rate, no longer than until the debt
caused by the campaign in Spain was discharged.
Some members assented to it; but a number of the
greatest barons protested against it; saying that when
assuming the lordship of Aquitaine, the prince had
sworn to maintain all the rights and privileges of its
nobles, who when they were vassals to the King of
France had no taxes, or duties to pay, nor were they
going to do it now,—they would fight first.   Nevertheless,
for peace' sake, they were willing when they returned
home, to give further consideration to the subject,
and take counsel concerning it with their neighbours.

Nothing more could be obtained from these resolute

barons of Gascony, for it was they, who were the dissen-
tients; so the parliament was broken up, to reassemble
on a certain day named by the prince. The more peaceable feelings of its insubordinate members, however,
evaporated by the time they reached their own castles
and fortresses, at whose grim walls many a glance was
doubtless cast, as their sturdy owners thought how they
might, in case of need, hold them out against their
lord. Pay the tax they would not,—those old castles of
theirs should smoke sooner than that; neither would they
return to the parliament, catch them doing *that.* But
there was one thing they would do, and this was, walk off
straightway to the King of France, tell him their troubles,
and appeal to him, as their sovereign lord, against the
oppressive doings of the Prince of Aquitaine.

Now this talk of appealing to the King of France
was a downright mistake of theirs. According to the
treaty of Bretigny, King Charles was no more sovereign
lord to them, than he was to the English nobles. In
it all right and jurisdiction over them had been formally given up. But in their anger it was not convenient to remember this, and Charles, to whom they
posted, was much too well bred to tell them they were
altogether in the wrong about it. Of course he, in
his secret soul, was well pleased with so charming an
opportunity of picking a quarrel with the prince, and
having the prince's own lords to back him in it. But
neither did he tell this to the Gascons. He told them

blandly that the prince's attempt to encroach upon
their rights and privileges, was most probably the
fault of ill-advisers in his court; nevertheless, all that
he himself could with propriety do for them should be
done willingly; he had sworn, as his father had done,
to several articles of peace with the King of England,
all of which, of course, (speaking off hand,) he could
not remember; but he would have them looked into,
and all the rights and privileges of the Gascon nobles, as
there established, he would readily help them to maintain. With that he royally bowed them out; so well satisfied with their answer, that they did not care to return
home.   They preferred remaining at Paris with so gracious a monarch, into whose willing ear they might pour
their complaints of the prince's pride and presump-
tion; and their assurances of his perfect competence
to settle the matter, spite of that formidable individual.

If the prince was displeased at the point-blank
refusal of these Gascon noblemen to pay the tax imposed upon the province, he was still more so at their
referring the subject of dispute to one who had really
nothing to do with it.   It was a positive insult to
himself.   They had no right of appeal; that, as has
been said, was given up when the twice-beaten French
were forced to surrender so large a portion of their
broad lands to the English; lands over which he now
ruled, subject only to his own father, as sovereign lord.
The hearth-tax he made up his mind to have; he was not

to be baffled by these insubordinate barons, nor that meddling French king. Such was the prince's mood.

Chandos, who was a wise, as well as a valiant man, and whose gray hairs had brought him greater experience in matters of state, than his valiant master could boast of, opposed the prince's persistence in this tax. He foresaw the dangers of it, and would fain have avoided them. Unfortunately the prince was not to be moved, and finding his interference useless, Sir John judged it best to retire from the court for awhile; that he at least, might not have the blame, of what he had done his best to prevent. So to give colour to his departure, he made the excuse of wishing to visit his estate of St. Sauveur, le Vicomte, in Normandy, (conferred upon him, for his great services, by King Edward,) which he had not seen for three years. And with Sir John out of the way, the prince went on demanding the tax, from the more manageable portion of his subjects, who were willing to pay it; rejoicing no doubt that he was at last carrying his point, spite of Chandos, and his over caution, and the insolent doings of those intolerable Gascons.

Those Gascons meanwhile, were still besieging the French king with their entreaties that he should judge between them and their prince; entreaties which they now enforced by threats of carrying their case elsewhere, to some other sovereign, if he refused them help. Charles, as we are aware, was all the time

longing to do as they wished him; but as he very well
knew that such a proceeding on his part would almost
inevitably end in war with England, he was obliged to
proceed very warily; not only in order to give some
appearance of right to what he did, but on account of
one of his brothers, the Duke de Berri, being still a
hostage in that country.

In this difficult and dangerous state of affairs, there
was not wanting a mischief-maker (one rarely is, where
he is least required,) to make ill worse.   The Earl of
St. Pol, one of the French hostages in England, having,
like his Grace of Anjou, distinguished himself by
breaking his parole, and sneaking away home, was
filled with an uncommon hatred of those whom he had
treated so shabbily, and of course was correspondingly
anxious to do them all the injury in his power.   With
this amiable motive (knowing full well that if the
prince were summoned to Paris, in character of a
vassal, it would inevitably produce a war,) he busied
himself in urging upon the French king a compliance
with the Gascon lords' request.   Others joined him in
this, including the Duke of Anjou, who, as has been
said, was in the same discreditable predicament as
himself, that of a breaker of his word.   Knights and
gentlemen held the keeping of their word, as one of
their most sacred duties; the breaking of it, as one of
the most dishonouring crimes of which they could be
guilty.   Hence it is pretty plain that though they

might be nobles, these two individuals were neither
gentlemen, nor good knights. However, such were
among the king's advisers; and all together, word-
breakers, and those not so disgraced, did their best to
persuade Charles of what he was very willing to believe,—that he was still feudal lord of the prince, and, as
such, had a right to summon him to plead before him.
They further made a fuss about the ill conduct of the
English since the peace was signed; and the result of
their advice and persuasions was the calling of a solemn
council to examine the various documents concerning the
treaty, and to deliberate on the best mode of action.

The prelates and nobles who composed the council
read, and re-read these documents, and thought, and
better thought over their contents, till they came to
the desired conclusion:—that the rights of the King of
France were invaded in Aquitaine, and that the English
had behaved so badly, that he would be justified in
making war upon them.

This opinion of his council was so agreeable to
Charles, that he received it very graciously, and determined to act upon it, as soon as it was safe for him to
do so. Accordingly, spinning out the time by telling
his impatient Gascon clients that though he should be
exceedingly sorry to drive them to any foreign lord to
seek the justice which they required at his hands, yet
such affairs called for much prudence and deliberation,
he set to work quietly, to sound these gentlemen as to

whether they were able to support him with any adequate force in case of war with the English. And as, beside paying the cost of their twelvemonth's residence in Paris, he also gave them presents of rich jewels (which gentlemen wore in those days, as well as ladies), we cannot be surprised at their vowing that they both could and would stand by him. In addition to these Gascons, some of the northern folks also protested that they hated the English (as well they might, seeing the English had so often ridden rough-shod over them), and were quite ready, if the opportunity were given them, to return to their old allegiance, and prove stanch Frenchmen.

So far so good. The train was being gradually laid, that was to blow the English to the moon,—or, at any rate, out of France. The next step in the process was now to be taken. A document was drawn up, as an appeal from the Gascon lords, to Charles, king of France, against the oppressions of the Prince of Wales, and praying the king that they might have justice done them. The wording of a document like this, which was to throw two kingdoms into a blaze, was rather a nice matter. Much scratching out, and interlining, and preparation of *very* rough drafts, took place before it was ready to be fairly copied, and sent to the prince, with an intimation that he must present himself in Paris, to answer the appeal before his lord of France, and abide judgment upon it.

It was done at last, and by way of giving it due effect, an "eloquent lawyer," and a "noble knight," were appointed to carry this impertinent document, and still more impertinent message, to the victor of Crecy, Poitiers, and Navaret.

The twain set out on their errand, and as, wherever they came, they announced themselves as the king's commissioners to the Prince of Wales and Aquitaine, they had no lack of civility on their journey. When they reached Bordeaux, where the prince and princess were then keeping their court, it was too late to seek an interview that day. So they remained for the night at their inn, going next morning to the Abbey of St. Andrew's, which was the prince's residence when in his capital city.

Finding they were messengers from the King of France, the courtiers received them very kindly; and when their lord was informed of the arrival of these envoys, he courteously ordered them to be at once conducted to his presence. After making their best bows to the prince, and opening their credentials, they respectfully delivered the impudent message with which they were charged; and which ended by bidding him use no delay in obeying the summons, but to set out to Paris, to have sentence pronounced upon him, as speedily as possible. It was dated at Paris, the 25th of January, 1369.

The prince heard it out quietly, and was silent for

awhile.   Then came his calm answer to this outrageous
insult: "We shall willingly come to Paris, since the
King of France desires it, but,—it shall be with our
helmet upon our head, and sixty thousand men at our
back!"

Down upon their knees dropped the two Frenchmen,
at this alarming reply, and began to beg and pray the
prince, for God's sake, to have mercy upon them.
They found out they had indeed put themselves into
the lion's den, and feared that in another moment they
should be gobbled up.   Tremblingly, they assured him
they meant no offence; they had only carried a message,
as any of his subjects would do for him, and they entreated that no responsibility of it might be thrown
upon their unfortunate shoulders.   The prince hastened
to assure them that he was not in the least angry with
them,—such small game was beneath his notice,—but
he was exceedingly angry with those who had sent
them on such an errand.   The king, he said, had been
ill-advised thus to meddle where he had no business.
Charles had nothing to do with quarrels between him
and his barons.   It was at his own peril that he had
thrust himself into them, and he should soon find out
that when Aquitaine was given up to the King of
England, all rights, and jurisdiction over it, were given
up at the same time, so that there was no appeal, save
to him.   If it cost a hundred thousand lives, the King
of France should be made to understand *that;* and

turning on his heel, he left them, thunderstruck by the explosion they had provoked.

Standing planted there, in stupid astonishment, some of the English knights present told them, in a friendly manner, that they had executed their commission very well, but they had better go home, for they would get no other answer than the one they had received. So the "eloquent lawyer," and the "noble knight," returned to their inn, not a little crest-fallen with their morning's adventures. Fright, however, had not taken away their appetites, for the historian has thought it worth his while to leave on record that they got their dinner, before packing up, and setting out back again with the tremendous answer they had received.

The prince had acted with becoming spirit in dealing with this insult from the French court; but it occasioned him much uneasiness, foreseeing, as he did, that war was its ultimate design; and that he, the old scourge and terror of France, was no longer the brilliant, vigorous leader of his brave bands, but a disease-stricken man, slowly sinking into his grave. Such considerations were enough to fill him with painful anxiety; and his feelings were shared by those about him. To their dull wits no better plan suggested itself than that he should have the "eloquent lawyer" and the "noble knight" put to death, by way of suitable recompense for the impertinence of which, poor wretches, they had been the medium. The hot zeal of these gentlemen, however, found no countenance from the prince, who yet was so incensed against the messengers, as well as their master, that when he heard they had left Bordeaux, on the road to Thoulouse, where the Duke of Anjou was, he inquired whether they had had any passports given them. Understanding that they had none, he desired that they should be followed, brought back, and thrown into prison for their pains; for, on re-considering the matter, he could not regard them as envoys from the King of France, but from his own rebellious vassals, and as such, of course, they had no privileged character. Above all, he could not endure that they should go straight to his old enemy the Duke of Anjou, and tell him how they had insulted the prince to his face.

Sir William le Moine, who was despatched on this errand, made such haste that he soon came up with the travellers; and, fancying, no doubt, that he was vastly improving upon his master's directions, instead of arresting them in the prince's name for bringing defiant messages from his rebellious vassals, he, to their utter horror, accused them of horse-stealing; as he pretended, on the complaint of the innkeeper with whom they had lodged. There was a pleasant thing for a couple of French gentlemen, who had just had the enjoyment of treating the great Prince of Wales and Aquitaine, as though he were any ordinary baron, to have so vulgar a crime as that of stealing a horse—

an innkeeper's horse, too—laid to their charge! Of course it was of no use for them to say that they had not done it. They were forthwith clapped into prison, some of their people being permitted to continue their journey, and tell the Duke of Anjou, if they thought fit, how the French king had dealt with the prince, and with what contempt his messengers had been treated.

Both king and prince now began to make preparations for war, and in the course of them sundry knights and nobles changed sides; some who had formerly served the prince now tendering their allegiance to the King of France, and some of his liegemen turning heart and soul to the English cause. The Free Companions were also divided, one party selling their hireling valour to the prince, while others had secretly made merchandise of themselves to the French. The first blood spilled in what was destined to be a long, and to the English, disastrous war, was by the refractory Gascons; who in revenge for the imprisonment of the king's messengers, (or rather, as the prince had said, of their own,) took up arms, and set upon a small troop of the prince's followers, under his High Steward, Sir Thomas Wake. It was a safe little adventure; the Gascons, numbering three hundred lances, were in ambuscade, so that the rout of sixty unsuspecting horsemen, was no very wonderful affair, though doubtless they plumed themselves upon it.

The prince was in a rage when he heard that the

Gascon lords had dared to attack his high steward; and he vowed to inflict severe punishment for the offence. With this view he recalled Sir John Chandos, from the quietude of his Norman estate, and that valiant knight was soon in the saddle at the head of a large company of men-at-arms and archers. With him was the Captal de Buch, as well as other nobles; and many hard blows were exchanged between them and the Gascon lords, sometimes to the advantage of one, sometimes to that of the other.

King Edward could scarcely believe that Charles intended fighting, and so did not take as much care as he might have done of his northern French possessions. While to gain a little more time, things not being quite ready for the grand crash, Charles sent envoys to England, to lodge all sorts of complaints against Edward and his son the prince. They managed to employ two whole months in this agreeable work, holding many conferences with the king, whom they sometimes put in a passion with their unreasonableness; but, of course, they did not come to any settlement of the quarrel, *that* not being their object.

At length when the King of France was aware that the war had already broken out in Gascony; that in the north, certain of Edward's subjects were only awaiting a convenient opportunity of betraying him; and that he himself had a numerous army, not only ready, but eager for war with the Prince of Wales; he thought

the time was come for him to throw off the mask.
The mode which he adopted for doing this was to send
a formal declaration of war to the English court; but,
either from impudence or ignorance, he actually sent
this important document by his own valet. It was a
dreadful blunder, and Edward and his council were not
a little offended at so gross an impropriety as sending
a declaration of this nature by such hands. They said
(and they were quite right) it was not decent that war
between two such great monarchs as those of France
and England, should be declared by a common servant.
Some man of rank, prelate or baron, would have been
more fittingly employed upon the errand.

It was well the poor valet had not to suffer for his
master's indiscretion. But he was civilly dismissed after
he had delivered his letters (of whose contents he protested his ignorance), and got away home with all speed.

King Charles, however, did a worse thing than even
this of offering an unworthy insult to his great rival.
After sending off his shabby messenger to the English
court, he sent that shabby St. Pol, and Sir Hugh de
Chatillon to Abbeville, which had been secretly won
over to the French, and whose gates being opened to
them, gave an example of defection which was speedily
followed by the whole province of Ponthieu, before the
reinforcements, ordered from England for the protection of the county, could arrive.

XIII

Treaty of Peace broken by the French.

AN old historian tells us that King Edward was in a "mighty passion" when he heard of these things. And certainly if anything can justify people's being in "a mighty passion," the craft, the successful craft, of King Charles was ample excuse for an utter loss of temper on the part of our great Edward. It was enough to provoke any one who had suffered and fought so hard for conquest, as he had, to have the fruit of that conquest *stolen* from him. Had Ponthieu been again the prize of him who could hit hardest and longest,—however ill it had befallen him in the contest, Edward could have borne it better. As the treaty was now broken by the French, he again, by advice of Parliament, assumed the title and arms of King of France,—a title and shield which have only of late years been erased from our coin. Till that period, every shilling and sixpence, handed over the meanest shopkeeper's counter in England, bore testimony to the iron hand with which, from time to time, we English

have stricken our neighbours over the channel in main-
tenance of a right claimed over them.   With the hearty
support of his Parliament, he further made preparations
for a tough struggle with that treaty-breaker, Charles
of France.   A military force under his third son the
Duke of Lancaster, and the Earl of Pembroke his son-
in-law, was at once ordered to the assistance of the
Prince of Wales; and thanks to the Duke of Brittany,
whose quarrels as Earl of Mountfort the English had
long espoused, permission was obtained to land these
troops at St. Malo, and march them through his
dominions to the seat of war.

A numerous body of those rough and ready fellows,
the Free Companions, was also brought to the prince's
aid by Sir Hugh Calverly; and being immediately appointed to execute summary justice on the leading
Gascon mal-contents, executed their commission in the
most satisfactory manner to their employer,—by plundering, burning, and otherwise destroying the lands of
these noblemen.   Thus England and France were once
more at war.   The monarchs of those two countries, it
should be added, not only fought but preached against
each other !   That is, they set their clergy to do it, and
on both sides the water these exerted themselves, in
their way, by " long and fine " sermons, setting forth
the justice of the quarrel, as actively as did the fighting men.   The exhortations of the clergy had much
influence on the French king's success.   In addition to

preaching up the justice of the war, which both kings required from their clerical subjects, Charles went so far as to go in solemn procession with his ecclesiastics, praying for the success of his arms.   And as, after the custom of those times when extraordinary devotion was intended, he walked shoeless and stockingless on these occasions, doubtless a still happier result was anticipated from his exertions.

Had Charles kept faith with the English, we might have felt more respect for his prayers.   But while we reprobate word-breaking, either by monarch or subject, it must be admitted that the temptation to free so large a number of his people from a foreign yoke, and himself from a continual humiliation, was very great; and those of us who never yield to temptation, even when it is most enticing and most convenient, are, perhaps, the fittest to pour unmeasured censure on the French king's doings.   Yet, with all our allowance for the vehement temptation presented to this sovereign, (or to any one else who proves false, when remaining true would injure him), we are not to forget that promises *must* be kept.   Had the morality of the Prince of Wales been of as loose a character as that of his opponent, the war might not have taken place; for, as we have seen, it was brought about solely by the imposition of that hearth-tax, which was forced upon the prince by his determination not to break faith with those to whom he had pledged his word.

Charles was not content with attacking and under-mining the English in France. He also fitted out an immense fleet, which, under the command of his brother, the Duke of Burgundy, was designed to invade and utterly destroy England. Not Napoleon himself, when he talked of driving us English into the sea, contemplated a more entire destruction of those terrible islanders than did he. Both, however, were doomed to disappointment in their glowing anticipation of victory. Between brisk preparations made for his reception on the other side the channel, and fresh work cut out for his troops by the arrival of the Duke of Lancaster in the north, Charles thought it best to give up his plan of attacking his old enemies upon their own shores; so that his fine fleet was of no use to him, the troops who should have gone on board it finding quite enough to do in watching the duke's army. Fighting they did not attempt, though far superior in number; being warned, by past experience, that pitched battles with the English did not agree with their constitution.

The first success of the French in this long, and to the English disastrous, contest, it has been said, was gained by craft. But it must be owned that when blows decided the matter (and some very hard ones were struck on both sides) they still had the best of it. Our time was come. Perhaps we had no business in France! And then there was no longer the Black Prince to meet the enemy in the field. He was too ill even to mount his horse; had he not been, Charles and his people would scarcely have ventured to stir in the matter. The prince, like Æsop's sick lion, was compelled, in his feebleness, to endure indignities which in health and strength none would have dared to offer him.

While the Dukes of Lancaster and Burgundy in the north were thus watching each other, as a cat would a mouse, things were going on more briskly in the south, to which we must now turn our attention. There small battles were fought, and castles besieged with varying success as fortune favoured, now the French and then the English. Chandos, the captal, Lord Audley—the Audley of Poitiers—and Sir Robert Knolles, were the principal leaders in this part of the country. Grief for the death of his son, however, caused Audley to retire from active service; and then Chandos, who was a tower of strength to his master, succeeded that nobleman as Seneschal of Poitou. In this character Sir John got together a strong body of English and Poitevins, with which he purposed making an excursion into Anjou to beat up the quarters of the French in that province; and as the young Earl of Pembroke was in garrison with two hundred lances at Mortagne-sur-mer, he sent for him to join the expedition. There was nothing that the earl would have liked better; but some mean souls about him suggesting that if he, who was but a young knight, went out in company with so old and experienced a commander as Chandos, the latter would have all the credit of the enterprise, his ardour cooled down rapidly, and he was easily persuaded that so great a man as he ought to act by himself, in order that all the world might know what a very clever fellow he was. So he declined Sir John's invitation, who consequently was obliged to go without him.

Sir John marched into Anjou, where, pitching his quarters in the plains, he sent out light divisions in all directions to destroy the neighbouring country, in which, during the fifteen days they remained there, they did "infinite mischief," as one may well believe. When there was no more mischief to be done, they set out on their return to Poitou. On arriving at Chauvigny, about eighteen miles from Poitiers, information was brought Sir John of the near neighbourhood of a large body of men-at-arms under de Sancerre, Marshal of France; and as he wished to attack him, he sent a second time to Pembroke, begging him to bring up his men. The foolish earl again refused, though the herald who carried the message found him mustering his men, as if for service; and as without him Sir John had not force sufficient to meet the marshal, he was reluctantly obliged to give up his purpose, and go straight to Poitiers where his followers dispersed.

As soon as Pembroke heard that Sir John had disbanded his troops, he thought that now (when he could have all the glory to himself) was the time for him to show of what sort of stuff he was made. So at the head of three hundred men-at-arms, whose numbers were increased by others as they passed along, he sallied out of Mortagne, and made his way into Anjou, apparently for the purpose of gleaning, where Chandos had been so ruthlessly shearing. Of course it was very pleasant for the little, great man to go about doing mischief on his own account, rather than at the bidding of the knight of Poitou. The mischief was his own, his very own; no chance of Sir John's getting the least bit of credit for it. But, alas! pride had a fall. The French did not think quite so highly of my lord as he thought of himself; Chandos they knew and feared, but the insolent young knight, whose vanity would not allow him to serve under that veteran, (they had heard the whole story), they thought they might manage to overthrow. To this end several of the French commanders laid their heads together, and concerted for the discomfiture of the brisk young earl. Collecting their troops they accordingly came stealthily on his track, and just as the earl's party had re-entered Poitou, and settled themselves, comfortably as they thought, in the village of Puirenon, in, about supper time, dashed the Frenchmen, making the dusky streets resound with cries of, "Our lady for Sancerre," and tilting away at every one they met. The uproar soon reached head-quarters, and the earl and his friends, arming in haste, came along with such of their people as they could get together to see what was the matter. But unluckily for them the French had, in this sudden manner, so completely got possession of the place as to render it impossible for the whole company to assemble. Separated, they were easily cut off, and, after many of them had been killed or taken prisoners, Pembroke and a few others were driven to take shelter in an ill-fortified house belonging to the Knights Templars, where they just contrived to save their precious selves; all the earl's plate being left behind as a trophy for the French.

It was rather humiliating for my lord, just as he was rejoicing in having got rid of the overwhelming superiority of the great Chandos, to find himself thus caught like a rat in a trap. But his worst humiliation was yet to come, as we shall see; and, however unpatriotic it may be thought, we cannot after all, help enjoying the troubles of this presumptuous young soldier.

As the French had no mind to be deprived of their prey, when it appeared to be within their grasp, they marched up to the house where our friends had taken refuge, and after examining it pretty closely, determined to attack it. Scaling ladders were accordingly brought, fixed against the walls, and, holding their shields over their heads to ward off stones and arrows from above, some bold fellows struggled up. But, as an old writer

says, when they had done that, they had not done
much, for on reaching the top of the wall, they met so
brisk a reception from the beleaguered knights, as sent
them to the bottom again, much quicker than they had
mounted; while such flights of arrows were poured in
upon those below, as made even that anything but a
comfortable post.

Time after time were these attempts made and re-
pulsed, until the deepening gloom of evening rendered
it impossible to renew them. Sounding their trumpets
for the retreat, the French then sheared off, in remark-
ably good spirits, saying they had done enough for one
day, but would try again on the morrow. For fear
lest the birds should be flown before morning,
they placed a strong guard in front of the house,
which they were determined to have, either by assault
or by starving out its garrison; and then they retired to their quarters where they "made a night of
it."

Being ill supplied with provisions as well as artillery, my Lord Pembroke and his friends were by no
means in so cheerful a frame of mind as that enjoyed
by the confident Frenchmen. They could, of course,
make shift to fast for awhile, but still after all, hunger
added to danger is anything but enlivening. And yet,
even this was better than what my lord had to come
to at last. It was very mortifying, after riding his
high horse with the veteran of Poitou; but in his pre-

sent strait there was no help for it; Chandos must be
sent for to help him out of the difficulty, into which
his own obstinate folly had got him.   So the beleaguered party managed to smuggle one of their number
out at the back door, with injunctions to ride for his
life to Poitiers, and entreat Sir John to come to their
assistance.   It was midnight when the messenger was
despatched, in hope of bringing Chandos to them by
next day's noon; but being unacquainted with the
country, he wandered about until it was broad daylight,
before he even found the road to Poitiers.   Meanwhile,
at peep of dawn, the French were at work again, climbing up their ladders, and getting the benefit of a wake-
ful night spent by the earl and his friends in adding
to their means of defence against these persevering
assailants.   Great stones and even ponderous benches
had been carried to the roof of the house, and thence
were now liberally bestowed upon the heads of the
besiegers below; while as before—the fight, hand to
hand, with such as scaled the wall, was as obstinate as
it possibly could be.

As the morning wore on, anxious glances were cast
on the road leading to Poitiers, in hopes of catching some
signs of the knight's approach for their rescue.   Not
even Bluebeard's sister-in-law "sister Anne," looked
out more eagerly for her brothers, than did those
English knights, under the unlucky leadership of Lord
Pembroke, for the advancing banner of Chandos.   But

no welcome "cloud of dust," announced that deliverance was at hand!

Between six and nine o'clock the French, tired of
climbing up their long ladders only to be knocked on
the head, or pitched to the bottom again after they got
to the top, sent off for pickaxes, mattocks and such
like tools, for the purpose of undermining the walls,
pressing some of the sturdy villagers around, into their
service for this congenial occupation. The earl was
alarmed (and hungry) before, but he was in a regular
fright now, for this was by far the most dangerous
trick the enemy had yet played him; and to hasten
Chandos to his aid, he sent off another squire, post
haste, out at the back as before, with his own ring as
a token, by way of convincing the old knight that it
was really he himself who wanted him. By this time,
however, the first messenger, who had wandered about
the whole night before finding the road to Poitiers, had
arrived in that city on his jaded steed; and hearing
that Sir John was at prayers (for, as we have said,
those warriors of the olden time, prayed as well as
fought), at once rushed in to him, dropped upon his
knees, and besought his speedy interference on behalf
of the young earl and his companions.

Sir John was justly piqued at Pembroke's double
refusal to join his expedition, so he took the matter
very coolly. "It was," he said, "almost impossible
to get to Puirenon time enough to serve the earl,

as prayers were not yet ended;" and so saying, he calmly went on with them again. When service was over, the tables were covered for dinner, and just as the seneschal was about to sit down, in came squire the second, who, like his predecessor, kneeling before the great man, presented his token, with an urgent request that Chandos would hasten to help the earl out of his pressing danger. Sir John took the ring, examined it closely, and seeing that it really was the earl's signet, remarked as before, very gravely, that if the danger were as imminent as described, it would be impossible for him to get to Puirenon in time; and therefore he ordered dinner to be served.

Oh, that the earl could but have *seen* the quiet contempt with which Sir John treated his petitions, instead of only feeling the consequences of it !

The stately household sat down to table, wondering, as they ate and drank, what possessed their master; but by the time the second course was brought up, Sir John began to think he had inflicted sufficient punishment upon the vain boy shut up in the Templars' house at Puirenon. Raising his head from his plate, they must have been dull who could not perceive the kindling glance of his eye, as he told them that the Earl of Pembroke, son-in-law of their lord, the King of England, entreated him for help so courteously that it behoved them at once to mount and be gone—if it were possible to arrive in time. Pushing the table from him as he spoke; he rose, saying: "Gentlemen, I am determined to go to Puirenon!"

The call to "boot and saddle," as the trumpets rang out their shrill note, was a joyful sound to his followers, who were soon armed and riding away with their master to Puirenon. News of this approaching succour speedily reached the French, who, little as they cared for Pembroke, were not (after some hours' hard fighting that day) particularly anxious to come in collision with the Seneschal of Poitou. "Dear lords," said some of their scouts, "look well to yourselves, for Sir John Chandos with two hundred lances, is coming from Poitiers with great haste, and greater desires to meet you." This piece of information settled the matter. They came to a unanimous conclusion that they had best be off with the spoil and prisoners, before worse came of it; and with trumpets sounding the retreat they retired, bag and baggage, from the siege of my Lord Pembroke and his companions.

The earl and his knights seeing their tormentors retire, took for granted that Chandos was on his way to their help, and that intelligence of his advance had reached the enemy. So they hastily took horse to go and meet him, some in their eagerness riding double. It was "hail fellow, well met!" when they came up with the seneschal; only Sir John was vexed at not being in time to fight the French after all.   And then, as there was nothing more to be done, they departed to their several quarters; the earl carrying his crest much lower than he did before he was obliged to beg and pray a simple knight to come to the rescue of so high and mighty a lord as himself.

The prince loved his brother-in-law Pembroke; but we may safely conclude that when that nobleman next presented himself at Angouleme, where the court then was, he received a satisfying portion of the royal invalid's best thunder and lightning, in return for the public exhibition of his own folly and incompetence, which he had chosen to make on this occasion.

The prince, languishing under mortal illness, had at this time other griefs additional to those of seeing his hard-won territories wrested from him; while he, in his disabled state, was forced to employ such prigs as Pembroke in their defence.   His mother, the "good Queen Philippa," the loving wife and parent, as well as the heroine, who, in her husband's absence, could defend his kingdom for him, was now lying upon her death-bed.   Her character appears to have been altogether admirable; one that, apart from natural affection, must have commanded the affection and esteem of such a man as Prince Edward.   We may believe the old historian, who tells us that her death was "right piteous to the king, her children, and the whole realm." She was taken ill at Windsor, and her sickness continuing so long and heavily that, as the same writer says, it presently appeared there was no remedy for it but death, she summoned the sorrowful king to her bedside that she might make some requests of him.

Putting her trembling hand from out her coverings she took his within it, and reminding him how happily and prosperously they had lived together for more than forty years—from early youth to age—she prayed that now she was about to leave him, he would fulfil her last wishes, which (after providing for her servants, her religious benefactions, and some other matters) were that, when he too should quit this changeful life, he should be laid by her side in the cloisters of Westminster. The king, with tears, promised all that she desired; and soon after, having commended him and her youngest son Thomas (who, poor boy, stood crying by her side) to God, she devoutly yielded up her soul into His hands; a soul which, as the same old historian relates, he firmly believes was, with joy, carried up to heaven by the holy angels, for her whole life had been pure, charitable, and good. She died on the 15th of August, 1369, in the fifty-seventh year of her age, and her remains were interred in Westminster Abbey; where, in due time, as she had desired, her weary, worn-out lord found his last resting-place by her side. The particular spot, close by the shrine of Edward the Confessor, had been marked out by himself, ten years before, as that in which his bones should be laid.

The death of Queen Philippa was greatly lamented at home, and it was a sad day when intelligence of it reached her people and children in France.   But they did not suffer grief to disarrange their grim battle array!

XIV

Incidents of the War—Death of Chandos.

THE war still dragged on its slow length. Nothing decisive was done, the tactics of the
French being still to avoid general engagements; while in the skirmishing, and attack, or defence
of towns and fortresses, that occupied several campaigns,
though victory sometimes inclined to the French, sometimes to the English, yet in the main, the English
cause continued steadily declining.

The death of Sir John Chandos, who, about this
time, was killed in a skirmish, was a heavy blow to
the English interest in France. Sir John had been
excessively irritated by the loss of St. Salvin, a town of
Poitou, which had been treacherously given up to the
enemy; and in his anger that such a thing should
have happened in his own province, vowed he would
have it again, by some means or other, and make its
inhabitants pay dearly for the insult they had put upon
him. Scheme after scheme for the recapture of the
town did he devise, but the vigilance of its new

governor, Sir Louis de Julien, who was not to be caught napping, proved too much even for the genius and bravery of Chandos. Though baffled, however, he was not discouraged; and resolving to make one more desperate attempt to regain it, he summoned the Poitevin nobles and knights, by whom he was much beloved, to attend him at Poitiers, on New Year's Eve, 1370. They came trooping at his call, and at the time appointed, he left that city at the head of three hundred lances; none, save the principal lords in his company, knowing what was the object of the expedition. They marched towards St. Salvin, and on arriving there about midnight, it was explained to them that their cold ride was for the purpose of retaking it. Dismounting, and giving their horses to their grooms, they descended silently into the ditch of the fortress and prepared to plant the scaling ladders which they had brought with them. All went right, and they would soon have made their way into the fort, among the sleepy and unsuspecting Frenchmen, when, as ill luck would have it, there came such a blast from the warder's horn, as made them suddenly pause in their proceedings, taking for granted that they were discovered. This, as it turned out, was a mistake; but believing it, and the success of the attack depending upon its being a surprise, there was nothing left for them, but to crawl out of the ditch again, as quietly as they could, mount their horses and ride off.

On arriving at Chauvigny, five or six miles distant,
as nothing more was to be done, the greater part of the
discomfited troops returned home, leaving their commander, with about a hundred lances in that town.
Sir John, who was too vexed to go straight back again,
was disposed to make a halt here, and as he stood, grim
and gloomy, warming himself at the kitchen fire of the
inn, Lord Thomas Percy, who had remained behind,
asked his leave to ride out with his men in search of
adventures.   Permission was granted, but he had not
been long gone when word was brought to Chandos that
the French had taken the field, and were on their road
to Poitiers.   Sir John did not at first much mind about
it; he was too thoroughly out of humour with his disappointment to care for a brush with them, and as he
thought his people could put them down without him,
he was not for stirring.   Second thoughts, however,
which in his case were not "the best," led him to change
his purpose, and mounting his horse he left Chauvigny
with about forty lances ; for at any rate he must return
to Poitiers, and might as well do it then as later.

They pursued their route leisurely by the river until,
as the day broke, they came within sight of their friends,
under Percy, and the French, dismounted, and lance in
hand, prepared to dispute the passage of the bridge at
Lussac which it was necessary for the latter to cross.

Riding up to the French, of whom he made very
light, Sir John, who was by no means amiable that

morning, began rating them soundly: "Do you hear, you Frenchmen," said he, "you are a rascally set, going about as you please, night and day, taking towns and castles in Poitou, as though the country were your own." And then, his passion rising as he spoke, "Sir Louis, Sir Louis, you and Carnet, (the French leaders) are too much masters. Here I have been seeking you this year and a half, and now I have found you, we will see which is the stronger. You say you have often wanted to see me. Here I am, look at me well, I am John Chandos, and if God please, I will now see what you are made of."

While Sir John was thus scolding a-main, one of the Frenchmen drew his sword, and setting upon an English squire named Dodenhale, gave him some such severe strokes that he knocked him off his horse. Hearing the noise behind him Sir John turned, and seeing Dodenhale on the ground, with several of the French laying upon him as hard as they could, was in a greater rage than ever. Angrily asking his men what they were about to suffer their comrade to be slain in that fashion, he lept from his horse, bidding them "dismount, dismount." In a trice they followed his example, the squire was rescued, and the battle began.

Sword in hand, with his banner displayed, Sir John advanced towards the French, who, seeing the mood he was in when he came up, had at once drawn close together, and prepared to engage. But alas, alas! that

January morning the ground was slippery with frost, and
the knight, trammelled with his flowing surcoat, slipped
on its glassy surface. Just at that moment a French
squire, James de St. Martin, levelled a lance at his blind
side, (Sir John had lost an eye while hunting five years
before) and the visor of his helmet being unfortunately
open it entered his face below the eye. The thrust was
made with a strong arm, and in stumbling, Sir John
bore upon the cruel weapon with such force that it
penetrated the very brain before it was wrenched out
again. He fell without a word, for it was his death-
blow, turning over once or twice in the extremity of
his agony. Seeing him down, his followers pressed forward like madmen to avenge their leader. De St.
Martin was soon run through both legs by one of Chandos' squires, while his uncle, Sir Edward Clifford, be-
striding the body of his valiant nephew, dealt around
him such lusty sword-strokes as effectually shielded it
from the enemy who were struggling to carry it off the
field. But spite of the furious bravery with which they
fought, the English were overpowered by the superior
force to which they were opposed, and most of them
were taken prisoners, Clifford still standing over, and
refusing to quit the dying man, whose almost lifeless
body he had so well defended.

If the French had only been able to mount at once,
they would now have carried off their prisoners, and
made a successful affair of it. But unluckily for them,

their servants who were holding their horses in the rear, taking fright at first glance of the advancing banner of Chandos, had ridden away with them, anxious to protect their own valuable persons, though at the expense of their masters, who were left in the lurch. The Frenchmen were sorely put out when they discovered this, for they knew that in that hostile district it would never do for them, wearied as they were with battle, to attempt to carry off their prisoners, and their own wounded, a-foot.

So they sent off two or three of their number to hunt up the horses and servants. While awaiting the return of these, what should they see but a body of more than two hundred Poitevins, who had turned out on purpose to seek them, and were coming up with flying banners, under the leadership of some of the great lords of the province. The tables were turned now with a vengeance. Without horses, toil-worn, encumbered with wounded and slain, beside their own prisoners, they had no chance of resisting this fresh troop. There was small time for deliberation, but in that brief space their resolution was formed. Pointing out the advancing knights to the English whom they had taken, they promised these their liberty on condition of their accepting their recent captors as prisoners, and defending them against the new comers : for some reason or other the Frenchmen very much preferred falling into the hands of the English, to being in the power of their

own countrymen of Poitou. The English willingly
consented to this bargain; so when the Poitevins galloped up, lance in rest, the Frenchmen, backing a little
out of the way, shouted to them, " Holla ! stop my lords,
we are prisoners already." The newly released English
confirming this, down sunk those threatening lance-
points, and the owners, finding their work done to their
hand, at once became peaceable.

But when they saw their seneschal lying there
speechless and wounded to death, their grief broke forth
in bitter lamentations : crying out, " Oh, Sir John
Chandos ! cursed be the forging of the lance that
wounded thee, and perilled thy life, thou flower of
knighthood !" They wept, they wrung their hands,
especially his own servants, as they thus tenderly be-
wailed him ; while the wounded knight, though sensible,
could only answer them with his groans.

His armour was removed very gently by his servants,
and then, supported upon the shields of his knights, he
was slowly carried to Mortemer, a fort not far from the
spot where this unhappy encounter had taken place.
It *was* an unhappy encounter for the English, for though
they brought back good store of French prisoners, that
was not to be set in the balance against the loss of
Chandos, who survived but one day and night that
terrible lance-thrust from a mere squire.

Thus fell, in a pitiful skirmish, one of the best and
bravest knights that England ever produced.

His death was universally mourned. When the sorrowful news was made known, the prince and princess, and indeed all his countrymen, were sad at heart, saying that now they had lost all. Even some of the most renowned French nobles lamented for him; for though they feared him, they honored him as a knight who, like their own Bayard of after years, was "without fear, and without stain." And had he but been made prisoner instead of being piteously slain, they had such reliance on his wisdom, and the esteem in which he was held by his lord, that they doubted not he would have made peace between France and England. That hope was at an end, now that he was in his grave at Mortemer, and there was nothing for it but "war to the knife."

The King of England, indeed, made an attempt at mediation by publishing letters, in which, having recited the oppressions complained of by the Gascon lords, he, as superior lord, declared his will that amends should be made them; and that a full pardon should be granted to such as having taken part with the French should now return to their allegiance. By way of balancing this act of grace for the insurgents, it was further set forth that any complaints which the prince or his people had to make against them should be equally redressed. But Edward was not successful in his peace-making; the wound was too deep to be healed by such remedies. Great part of the population were too thoroughly French at heart to care for being the prince's subjects at any price, and the tide of French conquest swelled still higher and higher against him.

About this time the castle of Belleperche, belonging to the Duke of Bourbon, was seized by the Free Companions belonging to the English; and as it was a most desirable stronghold, whence they might ravage the Bourbonnois, in which it was situated, at their leisure, they settled themselves here. It had the further recommendation of containing a most valuable prisoner; for as at the time they took possession of it the duke's mother (who was also mother of the French queen) made it her residence, the old lady, as well as the old walls, fell into their hands; and though it was not considered correct, in those days, to make prisoners of ladies, whether old or young, the Companions were too lawless a set to feel themselves bound by the rules of polite warfare. So they stuck to the old duchess like wax, as well as to her fine castle.

Both king, queen, and duke were excessively annoyed at having their mother a captive, and in such hands; but they were obliged to submit to it for a while, until the increasing success of the French arms enabled the duke to raise a large body of troops with which he hastened to her relief.

He "sat down" before the castle in due form, building a sort of strong wooden fortress for the shelter of his men at night, while the day was spent in skirmish-

ing with the garrison.   Among the weapons of offence,
provided by the duke on this occasion, were several
large machines, the artillery of those days, for hurling
huge stones and logs of wood; and with these he kept
up such a pelt, night and day, against his own walls as
nearly frightened his mother out of her senses.   With
towers falling and roofs crashing in around her, it was
no wonder that the poor old lady's nerves should be
somewhat shaken by her son's strenuous efforts for her
deliverance.   And to such an extent was this the case
that she sent repeated messages, begging him not to
knock down the castle about her ears in this fashion,
for she could not stand it; but to get her out in some
less alarming manner.   The duke was sorry for his
mother, of course he was; but he was much too good
a son to give the slightest heed to her entreaties, knowing full well that if he spared his mother's nerves it
would be at the cost of her liberty; so he kept thundering on as hard as ever.

The garrison at length began not to like it; nay, they
found themselves so harassed by this persevering duke
that they were obliged to implore succour from their
friends further south.   As the castle was too important
a one to be lightly given up, the prince ordered a rein-
forcement, under the Earls of Cambridge and Pembroke,
to march at once for its relief.   On their arrival at
Belleperche, these camped opposite the besiegers, who, in
their turn, invited aid from all such knights and squires

of their own party, as were anxious to distinguish themselves by deeds of arms; an invitation that added considerably to their numbers.

The two armies remained looking at each other for
fifteen days, and then the English commanders, tired of
doing nothing, sent a herald to the Duke of Bourbon,
inviting him to a pitched battle at any place he might
choose to name. This the duke, point-blank, refused,
sending word in reply that he was not going to fight just
to please them, neither would he quit his post until he
had retaken his castle of Belleperche. The rejoinder was
that since he would not fight he should, in three days'
time, between nine and twelve o'clock in the morning,
see his lady-mother placed on horseback, to be carried
off, and he might rescue her if he could. But not even
this threat moved the duke from his purpose. "Tell
your masters," said he, "that they wage a disgraceful
war when they seize an ancient lady from among her
servants, and carry her away prisoner; such a thing
was never before known." He went on to say that it
would certainly be very unpleasant to him to see his
mother carried off in that way; but they must do it if
they thought fit, and he must rescue her as soon as he
was able. The castle, however, they could not take
away with them, and that he *would* have. He would
fight them fifty against fifty if they liked, and the victors should have the castle.

The English were no more disposed to accept the

duke's proposal than he had been to close with theirs. So, as they had said, on the third day, at nine in the morning, the poor old duchess was set upon a handsomely caparisoned horse, and together with her ladies and servants, marched off in company of the whole army; which, with trumpets sounding and banners flaunting in the air, returned to Limousin, where their prize was detained for some time by the Companions who had first taken her and her castle.

An angry man was the duke when he saw his mother led off in this manner. And an angry man was the prince also with the whole affair. He did not wage war upon women, he said. It was a disgrace to his chivalry that he could not forgive, and never would have suffered on the part of his own people. Had *they* taken the duchess, she should instantly have been set at liberty. But those rovers, the Free Companions, were too little under control for him to interfere authoritatively in the case. Ungovernable, however, as they were, their regard for the prince led them speedily to accede to his scheme for ridding himself of the shame of keeping a noble lady in captivity. This was to exchange the duchess for Sir Simon Burley, one of his own knights, and the school-fellow of his early days, who had fallen into the hands of the French. So the duke got both his mother, and his castle back again; for he marched into the latter, as soon as the Companions marched out of it.

XV

The Sack of Limoges—The Prince returns to England.

HE death of Chandos, whose great name and great deeds had hitherto held the prince's disaffected subjects in awe, led to the falling away from their allegiance of several more of the Gascon and Poitevin lords. And as this necessitated increased efforts on the part of the English, to keep their heads at all above water, Sir Robert Knolles was summoned to England, to advise with the old king as to what was best to be done.

Sir Robert was joyfully received at Windsor, and one result of the anxious consultations held there was the raising of a large army, which, under the command of Sir Robert, was to land at Calais, and thence march through the country to the assistance of the prince, who was also to be joined by a tolerably respectable body of men-at-arms and archers, under his brother, the Duke of Lancaster.

The army under Sir Robert amounted to thirty

thousand men. They landed in safety at Calais; and, after a few days' rest in that neighbourhood, took their road southwards, plundering and destroying the country, or else despoiling the inhabitants by making them pay smartly to be spared. So terrible were Sir Robert's doings, that for many a long year afterwards the pinnacles and gable ends of ruined churches and houses in the district which he had laid waste, were known, in bitter jest, as "Knolles' mitres." In this style he marched along, until his destroying host made their appearance before the gates of Paris. The king, with the Constable of France, and a throng of nobles and knights, was in the city at the time; but, following his old successful policy of avoiding an engagement, he looked coolly on, while the fire and smoke of the enemy's ravages were daily visible to the affrighted citizens. It was not an easy thing for these French knights to lie there inactive, while all this destruction was going on; but the king's orders were imperative, and there was no contravening them. Charles was encouraged in his passive resistance by the Lord de Clisson, one of the most influential of his counsellors. "Sir," said he, "why should you employ your troops against these madmen? Let them go about their business; they can't deprive you of your kingdom, nor drive you out of it by smoke."

De Clisson was quite right. There was no driving Charles out of his own France, either by smoke or anything else; and, finding that he could not by such means provoke a battle, Sir Robert was forced to pass on his way towards the south.

Just as the English were breaking up their camp, and had, by way of leave-taking, set fire to as many villages round about as were yet unburned, there occurred one of those incidents that are so strikingly illustrative of chivalric notions in the middle ages. One of the English knights, tired out with having no opportunity afforded him of showing his prowess in arms, made a vow that he would, at any rate, advance as far as the barriers of the city, and strike them with his lance, as a parting insult to those intolerably forbearing Frenchmen. Accordingly, lance in hand, target slung round his neck, and completely armed, save his helmet, which, as customary, was carried by his squire, he rode towards the gates. On approaching them his helmet was laced on, and then, striking spurs into his good steed, he went prancing and curvetting right up to them. As they were open, it was thought he meant to enter the town; but that was not his purpose. Dealing the timbers a hearty blow with his lance, his vow was accomplished, and he then turned to rejoin his friends. The French lords and knights clustered about the walls looking on, applauded his spirit and courage, at the same time bidding him get away as fast as he could, for they were unwilling so "plucky" a fellow should come to any harm. But, though they generously let him alone, this adventure cost the knight his life, and that by very vulgar hands.

Riding back through the suburbs carelessly enough, for he had no thought of danger, he was met by a sturdy fellow of a butcher, who—with a heavy axe which he carried, one, doubtless, for knocking down oxen—struck the knight so violent a blow between the shoulders as sent him flat on his horse's neck. Just as he was recovering himself, a second blow on the head, cut through helmet and skull, causing him to drop senseless out of the saddle; while his terrified horse galloped off at once to the spot where the squire was awaiting their return. Seeing the horse come back riderless, the man set off in alarm to look for his master, whom he found lying there, with four fellows pounding away at him as though they were hammering an anvil, and who soon beat out of him what little life had been left by the butcher's axe. At this sight, the squire, frightened for himself, fled as fast as he could, and the poor knight, whose foolhardiness had brought him to his end, being killed outright in this horrible fashion, received honourable interment from the French lords, by way of testifying their admiration of his boldness; for in those days such rash and foolish deeds were held in great esteem—valour was honoured for its own sake: people did not always stop to inquire whether it was tempered by discretion. The knight's English friends were, of course, angry enough; not at their comrade's folly, but at their losing him by the hands of a pitiful butcher. It was in their eyes anything but a respectable end for so valiant a knight; and so it must be owned is it in ours!

Leaving Paris behind him, Sir Robert pressed on towards the prince, but with diminishing forces; for some of the lords and knights under his banner took to quarrelling among themselves, and with their brave commander also, because, forsooth, they were much too great men to serve under a simple knight. The truth was that Sir Robert, who was of mean parentage in Cheshire, had raised himself from the ranks,—as we should phrase it in these days,—having entered the army as a common soldier during King Edward's French wars; and that illustrious monarch, who knew a good soldier when he met with one, had advanced him, solely on account of his valour, to his present deservedly high position. There was among these captains one special mischief-making gentleman, who, it is supposed, had been bought by French gold; and he ended his grumbling by deserting with a large body of men: a piece of treachery that afterwards cost him his head. This was a severe blow to Sir Robert's army, but a worse was to follow. Du Guesclin, who had been fetched from Spain and created Constable of France, collected a large force, which he led out to that part of the country where the army of the north was moving about, with the intention of fighting, when they

two met. Sir Robert, hearing of his approach, thought
it best to be beforehand with him, and as his companies
were scattered, sent orders to their various captains to
join him that he might attack the constable. Unfortunately, before the junction could be effected, du
Guesclin fell in with one of these detachments, and a
sharp engagement ensued, in which, though the English stood their ground valiantly, they were entirely
defeated, every man of them being either killed or
made prisoner.

His army being thus broken up, it was impossible
for Sir Robert to reach his destination in the south.
The only thing left for him was a retreat to the friendly
province of Brittany, where his people dispersed in
different directions, some taking service with other
commanders, while the remainder, whose zeal for com-
bating the French had evaporated, went quietly back
again to England. What sort of reception they met
there, we are not told. It may be supposed not to
have been a very enthusiastic one.

Du Guesclin treated his brave prisoners very courteously, allowing them to go at large, on parole, until
they could procure their ransoms. He was a brave
man himself, and therefore knew how to respect valour
in others.

While these things were going on in the north, the
poor sinking prince was stung into a last effort to
grapple with his enemies in the south. The Dukes of

Berri, and Anjou, brothers of the French king, with
each of them a formidable army at his back, marched
towards Aquitaine, with the ultimate intention of joining their forces, and besieging the prince himself in
Angoulême. They moved onwards, each in his route,
taking cities and castles on their way, until the whole
country was alarmed, and the prince, vowing his
enemies should never find him shut up in town or
fortress, but that he would, as of old, meet them in
the open field, determined to give them battle in person. From far and near his loyal subjects were summoned to attend him ; and the rendezvous being fixed
at Cognac, on the Charente, he proceeded thither with
the princess, and their second son Richard, then a child
of five years old.

Meanwhile the Duke of Anjou had advanced as far as
Linde, a town situated on the Dordogne, and occupied
by a strong garrison under a Gascon knight, named
Sir Thomas de Batefol. The duke, who had a mind
to take this town, ordered his forces before it, planted
his battering machines, and prepared to besiege it in
due form : Linde, he vowed, he *would* have, he would
not stir a foot until he had made it his own. At the
same time he contrived to make the inhabitants understand that if they submitted to him quietly, it would
be decidedly the more comfortable plan for all parties.
The people of Linde were anxious to follow the example
of the other revolting towns, and as the duke's fine

promises to them were backed by still finer ones of handsome bribes to the governor, who was to have so much down and a pension for life, the whole affair was very neatly arranged between them : the gates were to be opened, and the duke was to take peaceable possession of the town.

If a secret, however, be communicated to many persons (as this shameful one had, of course, to be), it is apt to ooze out; and so it was in the matter of the treacherous surrender of the good town of Linde. It is not known who was the leaky individual, but the fact is that the whole arrangement was made known to the Earl of Cambridge, who commanded at Bergerac, about three miles off, the very night before it was to be carried out.

The news came like a thunder clap ; but there was just time to disappoint the contracting parties. The captal, and Sir Thomas Felton, who were with the earl, declaring they would be present at the surrender of the town, immediately set off thither with a considerable body of troops. Arriving at day-break, they commanded one of the gates to be opened, and riding right through the town, never drew bridle till they reached the opposite one, before which the French were already crowded, awaiting its being thrown open by that disreputable Sir Thomas, who was there to admit them. The traitor had made a good bargain for himself, but he did not live to enjoy it. The captal, springing from his horse, sword in hand, fell upon the knight,

and, sternly telling him he should commit no more
treason, ran him through the body with such force that
the point of his weapon came out on the other side.
The French fled at sight of the captal and Felton, and
the town was saved for the time. The inhabitants
were, of course, dreadfully frightened lest they should
suffer for their share in the transaction ; the speedy
justice done on their governor, who lay there a dis-
honoured corpse, leading them to apprehend the worst
for themselves. But as they made a profusion of
apologies, and threw the whole blame upon the dead
man, who, of course, could not answer for himself, they
got off better than they deserved; though the captal
and Felton judged it expedient to remain in the town,
to secure their good behaviour, as long as the Duke of
Anjou camped in the neighbourhood.

It was just at this time that the French leaders became aware of the prince's design to take the field
against them in person; and, feeble as he was known to
be, such was the terror inspired by his mere name, that
even the great du Guesclin advised that they should,
for the present, be content with what they had done,
and retire, leaving garrisons in the numerous towns
that had already transferred themselves to the French,
or been seized by them. The prince, it was thought,
could not last long, and when he was gone, they might
have their own way of it.

As the Duke of Anjou entered the prince's territories

by the way of Toulouse and Agen, the Duke of Berri
brought his troops into the Limousin, where, after
doing much mischief, he laid siege to the city of
Limoges. The Bishop of Limoges was one in whom
his lord, the prince, placed great confidence, of which,
as it afterwards turned out, he was utterly unworthy ;
for, while the Dukes of Berri and Bourbon were lying
before the city, he secretly entered into a treaty to
deliver it up to them. This was easily effected, as,
owing to the prince's trust in the bishop, a very small
force of English, under Sir Hugh Calverly, had been
deemed sufficient to garrison Limoges; and the inhabitants, being joined by their treacherous prelate, soon
overpowered Sir Hugh and his men. The gates were
then opened to the French, who marched in with much
parade, rested themselves for three days, and then, as
the Duke of Anjou had done, beat a retreat, retiring
each one to his own post, and leaving a hundred men-
at-arms, under three French knights, to guard their
new and important acquisition.

The prince was in a rage when he heard of the trick
his friend the bishop had played him ; and he swore by
the soul of his father—his most solemn oath—that he
would have Limoges back again, the very first thing
he did, and punish its slippery citizens severely.

Fair means were tried to begin with. The prince
sent heralds to the delinquents, with his commands that
they should return to their duty, and deliver up the

bishop to him.   But, trusting to their strong fortifications and garrison, the citizens contemptuously refused to do either the one or the other.   A more peremptory summons was next conveyed to them, accompanied by a threat of pulling their city down to the very ground, and putting all its inhabitants to the sword, in case of disobedience.   But this had no better effect than the former—nay, the herald himself, a privileged person, was treated with insult, and his master was set at defiance.   Upon this the prince immediately left Cognac with a large body of cavalry, archers, and other foot soldiers, having a grand array of lords and knights with him, among whom were his brothers, the Duke of Lancaster, and the Earl of Cambridge.   His brother-in-law, Lord Pembroke, was also one of the party.

The prince, still so weak that he could not sit on horseback, was carried in a litter during this march. On camping before the guilty city, he vowed he would never quit his ground until it was at his mercy; and seeing the determination of their powerful enemy, the bishop and his friends began to repent very heartily of having got themselves into such a scrape.   Repentance, however, came too late; they had not now the power, if they had the will, to deliver up the city, for the Frenchmen were masters of it, and they made very light of the fears both of bishop and people; assuring them they would undertake to deal with the prince who, spite of his threats, should do no manner of harm to Limoges.

It was all very well for them to talk largely in this way; but they sang a different tune before long.

A careful examination of the city and its defences, convinced the besiegers that they had little chance of carrying it by storm. So far the garrison were right; their fortifications were strong enough to keep out the prince. But there are other ways of getting behind stone walls, beside clambering over them, or beating them down; and the prince, in whose warlike expeditions, a strong corps of those useful fellows, we moderns call "sappers and miners," was always to be found, decided to attempt its capture by mining.

For a month or more, the miners kept steadily at work. The prince would not even be tempted into skirmishing with the hostile troops; that would have been agreeable enough to the knightly feelings of both sets of combatants, but it would not have contributed to the end he had in view, which was to lay that insolent city at his feet. For this purpose, humble pick-axe and mattock were better adapted than more chivalrous weapons; and the prince, who was a great general, as well as a brave soldier, was not to be led astray by brilliant achievements which conduced nothing to the final result of his campaign. Self-denial is one of the essential qualities of a good soldier. Such fool-hardiness as that of the knight who ran all sorts of risk in fulfilment of his vow to strike the barriers of the city of Paris, is a military vice, not a military virtue.

(3) 16

The prince was busy, and the garrison was not idle; but spite of their countermining (for mining is a game that two can play at), at the end of the time mentioned, his men had got on so well that they reported their readiness to throw down a large portion of the wall, whenever their commander thought fit to have it done. Six o'clock next morning was the time fixed upon; and at that hour, the combustibles with which the mine was filled, being set on fire, down toppled so great an extent of grim stone wall, that the ditch was filled with it. This formed a capital causeway for the English troops. They strode rapidly over it, and passing through the breach, soon beat down the gates and barriers with their heavy and sharp axes.

The suddenness of the attack added to its success. The besiegers, headed by the prince, his brothers and other commanders, rushed into the town, and as he had sworn, took terrible vengeance on the affrighted inhabitants. It was a sad business; the once humane and generous prince was indeed now "cruel," as he had always been "courageous as a lion," and heedless of entreaties for mercy, three thousand men, women, and children paid with their lives for the crime of their treacherous bishop.

How the prince should have so changed is inexplicable; but changed he was, fearfully, when he could sanction this horrid slaughter. He had been keeping bad company, with Pedro the cruel, of whom this evil

deed was more worthy than of him who had stayed the
hand of that monster, after the battle of Najara.
Excuse for the prince there is none, nor do we care to
seek it. Possibly the irritation of long continued, dis-
qualifiying illness, at a time when he must have been
panting to be in the saddle, once more leading his
valiant few to victory, against the swarming armies of
France, added to indignant anger at the base conduct
of the bishop and citizens of Limoges, may in some
degree account for this unwonted outbreak of the evil
passions of our human nature. And it must not be
forgotten that, five centuries ago, death, and human
suffering were much more lightly thought of than they
are now.

One party of the besiegers hastened to the epis-
copal palace, and seized the prelate, the real cause of all
these horrors. He was dragged with little ceremony
before the incensed prince, who flashing his angry
eyes upon him, answered his prayers for mercy by
assuring him he should lose his head for his pains;
and so saying, he at once ordered the culprit from his
presence.

The three French knights whom the Duke of Anjou
had left to defend the city, seeing the state of affairs,
drew up their men in good order, with an old wall at
their backs to protect their rear, and resolved, like
brave soldiers, to sell their lives as dearly as possible.
They were attacked heartily by the prince's brothers,

Lancaster, Cambridge, and Pembroke ; who advancing on foot set upon them so stoutly that notwithstanding the gallant defence of the Frenchmen, their men were all slain or taken.   The three royal brothers matched themselves singly against the three French knights, and the fight between them was so well maintained that the prince himself (who was still borne in a litter), drew near to watch the combat, for pure love of feats of arms.

Personal valour, however, was now unavailing to retrieve the day's disasters, and having done enough for honour, the Frenchmen gave up their swords in token of surrender.   But though they could not rescue the doomed city, their gallantry had its reward ; for the prince, who had been looking on, was so delighted with the prowess of these knights, that for their sakes he stopped the murderous work that was going on in the city.   Limoges, was of course, given up to plunder ; and when the English had pillaged it to their heart's content, they set it on fire, drawing off afterwards, with their spoil and prisoners, to Cognac again.

The guiltiest man in that unfortunate town, fared the best.   The bishop did not lose his head, as the prince had promised him, and as he verily deserved to do. His escape is said to have been owing to the friendliness of the Duke of Lancaster, who asked his brother to place the prisoner in his hands, under pretence of seeing execution done upon him.   Instead of that, however, the duke suggested to the pope that he should intercede for the bishop's life; and as a request from the pope could not well be refused, the prince ordered that the offender should be given up, though, it is said, at the same time he regretted that the prelate's head was not off before the arrival from Rome, of this unpleasant "begging-letter."

As winter now approached, the time for campaigning was at an end; so the prince's army was disbanded, and sent into quarters for that useless season.

The siege of Limoges was our hero's last campaign. His next battle was to be with an enemy that never yet was known to spare; and who finally bears down the best and the bravest: *Death* had been menacing the prince in the distance, and was now gradually drawing nearer and nearer, for the final struggle. Before striking down the gallant father, however, his cold hand closed upon the innocent son; or rather let us say, God, Whose servant death is, took that innocent child to himself.

In a few months after his return from Limoges, worn and exhausted with battle, and saddened doubtless by the unwonted cruelty into which his angry feelings had betrayed him—cruelty so unlike him—the prince lost his eldest son Edward, a boy of seven years old. The poor child died at Bordeaux, in the early part of the year 1371, to the great affliction of his parents and the whole court.

The prince now took the advice of his physicians to return to England on account of his health, as his native air might, it was thought, restore him. Previous to his setting sail from Bordeaux, he gave up the poor remains of the once stately province of Aquitaine, to the care of his brother, the Duke of Lancaster. All the barons and knights of the principality who continued faithful to their allegiance were summoned to Bordeaux to take leave of their prince, and do homage to his successor. Being assembled in the hall of audience, the prince told them that so long as his health had permitted him, he had striven to be a good lord to his vassals, and to defend them from all their enemies. Now he was compelled to leave them, and he besought them to be as loyal and obedient to his brother, as they had been to him. They willingly pledged themselves to this, and in token of their fealty (as was the manner of those times), kneeling before the duke, placed their hands between his, and kissed him.

The fleet that was to convey the prince to England was now awaiting him in the Garonne; and he went on board as soon as this important ceremony was at an end. His wife, and now only son Richard, were with him, as well as his two step-sons; and favourable winds speedily landed them in safety at Southampton. Two days' rest for the invalid were needful here; and then his stalwart knights and attendants taking horse, while he himself was obliged again to have the unwonted indulgence of a litter, the cavalcade moved on to Windsor, where the king received his great son very tenderly. After a short time had been spent there, the prince took up his residence at his Manor of Berkhamstead.

XVI

The Death of the Prince.

AFFAIRS went on from bad to worse after the prince's departure from Aquitaine. Skilful commanders, valorous knights, stout men-at-arms, were all in vain; there was no stemming the current of popular opinion, which flowed on steadily, in favour of converting that English principality into a French province. It is no easy matter to crush out nationality; and this was the task that King Edward had set himself to perform in the south-west of France, and in which he was thus signally discomfited. One after another the Gascon lords who had sworn allegiance to the prince's brother, as his deputy, quietly transferred that allegiance, together with their own lands, to the French king, and there was no power to punish their bad faith. These things were by no means exhilarating to the princely invalid in his retirement at Berkhamstead. That under such circumstances he could entirely refrain from chafing and fretting over his own enforced inactivity, was not to be expected;

and his anxiety and vexation contributed to disappoint the hopes that had been entertained of the beneficial effects of a return to his own country. Sweet English air could not counteract their influence.

The Duke of Lancaster, had been left behind in Aquitaine, but he presently got tired of his post, and threw it up. He had meanwhile married the eldest daughter of the late King Pedro, being advised by his courtiers that it would be a charitable act on his part to "comfort" the princess in this particular fashion; advice which he took, seeing that in return for his "compassionate" deed, he acquired a claim to the throne of Castile, when King Henry could be got out of the way. The Earl of Pembroke was appointed governor of Aquitaine in the duke's place. He had made himself liked in the province, spite of his nonsense about that expedition of John Chandos', and great things were expected from him when he came to rule the turbulent Gascons. Like many other great expectations, however, they were doomed to be disappointed. When the earl's fleet had arrived off Rochelle, on the 22d of June 1372, he found the port blocked up, by a large naval force, which, ostensibly belonging to the Spaniards, had in reality been sent thither by the King of France, acting in concert with Henry of Castile, who, no doubt, greatly enjoyed thus plaguing his old enemies, the English. A terrible battle ensued between the two, for the Spaniards were numerous, and the English.

though few, were full of spirit.   But neither spirit nor obstinate valour could avail against superior strength, and the use of a new and terrific means of destruction. Fire-ships, it is said, were first used in this sea-fight; by their agency thirteen of the largest English vessels were burnt, and after two days' hard work of it, the English were totally defeated, the earl himself, together with many of his best knights being taken prisoners.

The state of feeling in the prince's town of Rochelle, may be understood from the circumstance of its inhabitants looking quietly on while this fatal battle was being fought, and never attempting to render the least assistance to their fellow subjects, though earnestly urged to do so by the governor, and some other brave knights who were with him.   After this, we cannot be surprised to find the Rochellers presently transferring themselves and their city, in a formal manner, to Charles of France, having first had the precaution to make particularly good terms for themselves.

The Spaniards were so set up with having managed to beat the English, and at sea too, that they were perfectly riotous in their joy, during the day or two of their remaining at anchor before Rochelle.   Then, on the afternoon of the 24th, when the tide was at flood, with colours flying (pennons floating from their mast-heads, of such length, that they sometimes dipped in the undulating waters), and a prodigious ".row" of drums and trumpets, they sailed off to their own coast of Galicia, carrying with them the earl, and their other unfortunate prisoners, who, according to the barbarous Spanish custom of that day, were chained like criminals as soon as they were put on shore.   The earl was subsequently ransomed, but died on his way home.

King Edward was almost overwhelmed when news of the destruction of his armament, and the capture of Pembroke, reached England.   It was more vexation also for the prince, who had already had the grief of losing the captal; that gallant commander being taken prisoner in a skirmish before the castle of Soubise, to which the French had laid siege.   The captal, as constable of Aquitaine, was the prince's right hand; and the French greatly rejoiced when once they had got him strictly guarded within the walls of the temple at Paris.   Misfortunes, it is said, never come single. They were "thick and threefold" just now, for in addition to these two serious ones, a third provoking humiliation fell to the lot of the English monarch and his son.   Evan, of Wales, supposed to be son of one of the Welsh princes whom Edward had put to death, entered heart and soul into the service of the French king, in order to revenge his own losses of parent and territory.   At the head of four thousand Frenchmen, he attacked the English in Guernsey, beat them soundly, and would have damaged them still further had he not been recalled by Charles to more important service in France.

Towards the end of August in this same year there was so much amendment in the prince's health that he resolved to join a new expedition, which the king was fitting out against the obstinate Gascons and their abettors. He was growing desperate, and vowed, that he would now either retake all that he had lost, whether it was by treachery, or honest fighting, or lose all that remained.

The immediate occasion of this expedition was the condition of a considerable number of the king's faithful subjects, who being besieged in Thouars, by du Guesclin, were reduced to such straits as compelled them to promise to surrender, if after communicating their distress to King Edward, he should be unable to succour them before a certain time, Michaelmas in that year. The army got together for this purpose was a very large one; a special summons being issued, commanding that all persons throughout the kingdom, capable of bearing arms, should present themselves, properly equipped at Southampton, where four hundred vessels were moored to carry them across the seas. Previous to embarkation a solemn assembly was held at Westminster, where Richard of Bordeaux, the infant son of the prince, was duly acknowledged as successor to King Edward, in case, (as was too likely) the prince should die before his father.

The king, his sons, then the great barons of the realm, swore to maintain the rights of young Richard, and the love that the whole people of England had for the prince, caused this to be a very popular measure.

This weighty business settled, the king and his sons went on board, and the fleet left Southampton, for Rochelle, where it was intended to land the army. But there was now no break in King Edward's ill fortune. Those propitious winds that were wont to carry him over to the shores of France no longer filled his sails; and after beating about for nine weeks, they were reduced to the humiliating necessity of sailing back to England without striking one stroke in defence of the few possessions in France that still remained to the English. They had a spanking breeze to take them home again! Oh, if it had but blown in the right direction!

The army was disbanded on reaching shore, for it was now of no use; and Edward grumbled out that there never was a king who had fought so little as Charles of France, nor one who had ever given him more trouble. The "passive resistance" system had served Charles well.

After this unlucky termination of the expedition, the French king required the fulfilment of their promise from the knights pent up at Thouars; and they had no excuse for refusing it.

It might have been expected that the Duke of Brittany, whose quarrels the English had espoused zealously, and with so much success, would have proved

a valuable ally to them during their declining fortunes
in France.   The duke would fain have been so, he
would have liked to help them, actively, instead of
passively only.   Gratitude impelled him to this course,
for he said, that "such as he was, the English and their
king had made him, he owed everything he had to
King Edward."   But his people were so thoroughly
French, that he dared not stir in favour of his old patrons.
In fact his nobles, in the most polite and friendly
manner in the world informed him, that if he sided
with the English, they would throw him overboard
immediately; so their "dear lord," as they called him,
had to keep quiet, and swallow his vexation as he best
could.

   This fruitless voyage to Rochelle, is almost the last
glimpse that we have of the Black Prince.   Hopeless of
ever regaining health and vigour enough for active duty,
he formally resigned the principality which his father
had conferred upon him, and which was rapidly slipping
away from under English rule.   He was too feeble even
to take any conspicuous part in home affairs; though
there, as well as abroad, were disorders, which he, in
his better days, might and would have remedied, and
which must sorely have oppressed his spirit in the melancholy seclusion of his Hertfordshire home.   The old
king, doubtless in his dotage, did things that not only
lowered him in the esteem and affection of his subjects,
but also excited their strong discontent, which parlia-

ment took the liberty of expressing pretty plainly. His ambitious son, John of Gaunt, the Duke of Lancaster of this story, took advantage of the king's failings to lay hold of more power than fairly fell to him, and this again added to the public uneasiness; while the prince, who might have ruled all hearts in his father's dominions, was obliged to look, helplessly, on, capable only of suffering, not of acting. Once only the expiring flame leaped up, and the prince, spite of his overwhelming malady, repaired to Westminster to see justice done on some of his brother's creatures who had abused the king's authority entrusted to them, to the oppression of his subjects. One of these gentlemen, not knowing with whom he had to deal, thought to bribe the prince with a thousand pounds, concealed in an innocent looking fish-barrel. But it was indignantly sent back; with an intimation that the offender must bear the consequences of his misdeeds: as "he had brewed so he must drink."

The end came at last; not such an one as might have been expected for the hero of Crecy, Poitiers, and Najara. Death on the battle-field, so coveted by the knights of that period, as the most glorious that could befall a soldier, was not the fate of him, the best soldier of them all. Consumed by relentless disease, he was to meet, and succumb to, his last enemy on that sorrowful couch at Westminster, and the time was immediately at hand. On the 7th of June, of the same year, 1376, in which, spite of increasing illness, he had made himself a terror to the evil doers, who had imposed upon the old king's imbecility, a fresh accession of his malady put an end to all hope for his important life, and compelled his attendants to apprize their master of his rapidly approaching doom. The announcement was one for which he was not unprepared; his sufferings had been patiently, and religiously endured, and now he sedulously addressed himself to the last duties of a Christian man. His worldly affairs were first set in order, in a manner that showed his appreciation of those who had faithfully served him; and this occupied much of the short remaining time of him to whom time was about to be no more. The next day was Trinity Sunday, a festival which the prince had always been accustomed to observe with especial solemnity; and he broke out into a pathetic prayer that as he had ever loved that holy day, and caused others to celebrate it with him to the honour of the Blessed Trinity, he might now be at once called to his rest to keep the festival in Heaven with Him to Whose glory it was dedicated. Tokens of good will were then distributed to those around him, and a solemn charge given to his little son, soon to be King of England, that he should see his father's will in these matters religiously respected.

A painful incident followed. The prince feeling his last hour draw near, had commanded that his door should be closed to none, not even to the meanest page of his household; and among the sad and sorrowful throng who presented themselves, came one whose motive for entering that awful chamber, it would not be easy to divine. This was Sir Richard Stury, one of those evil doers for whose just punishment the prince had thrown off the lethargy of mortal illness, but who knew right well that though already condemned for his misdeeds, he need fear no penalty when once the ghastly form before him was motionless upon his bier.

The prince was at this time in his death-agony, yet seeing the villain advance, he bade him draw near to behold that which he had long desired to see; and when Stury vehemently affirmed that he had never desired the death of the prince, the dying man repeated his charge, adding that the fellow's own conscience assured him that so long as the prince lived, his evil deeds would never go unpunished; now his righteous avenger was going whither God called him, and to Him he remitted the wrong doer, praying that He would put an end to his "evil deeds."

Stury, penitent or rather perhaps over-awed for the moment, wept and prayed the prince to pardon him. But the latter too well knew the value of his penitential tears: "God that is just," said he, "reward thee according to thy deserts; I will not that thou trouble me any longer; depart forth of my sight not hereafter to see my face again!"

17

The agitation of this cruel disturbance of his last moments shook out the few remaining sands of the prince's life. Seeing him near his end, the Bishop of Bangor earnestly exhorted him to forgive his enemies, and to crave pardon alike from God and man for all his offences against them; but, faint and breathless, the prince could but respond by a feeble "I will, I will," often repeated. With well-meant, but pitiless pertinacity, the bishop told him that was not sufficient, he must deliberately express his forgiveness, and hope of mercy for himself. For one short moment the deathly languor passed away; and then, with folded hands and eyes raised to heaven, the prince solemnly gave thanks to God for all His mercies, beseeching Him to pardon his offences, and desiring forgiveness of all men whom he had himself offended.

They were his last words; his morning prayer was granted, and before the close of that Trinity Sunday his spirit had passed away to keep, as we may well believe, more high and holy festival in the immediate presence of that glorious Trinity Whom he had honoured upon earth.

Edward, the Black Prince, was but in his forty-sixth year when he thus died, to the inexpressible grief of the whole nation which had once looked forward to the wise, just, and glorious reign of one, renowned for valour and goodness, throughout the known world; and on whose manhood there rested but that sole stain of

DEATH OF THE BLACK PRINCE.

Page 269

the Sack of Limoges. A stain it was, and a deep one. No excuse can be found for it. Perhaps, as has been said, it may be accounted for, by his own peculiar circumstances of intense provocation, and the long continued irritation of disqualifying illness during a period which imperatively called for the most vigorous exertion both of mind and body.

He lay in state for some days at the palace, where vast numbers flocked to take a last look of one, so beloved and honoured, that even in France, by royal command, a solemn funeral service for him was performed in presence of the king and his chief nobility. His funeral finally took place, with much pomp and real mourning, in Canterbury Cathedral; the long, attendant train passing, sad and slow, through the city where, nineteen years before, the glittering cavalcade that welcomed the victor of Poitiers, had held its triumphant march. A stately marble monument still existing, was erected over his remains. There may be seen the recumbent mailed figure of this mighty prince, with the hands, according to the touching fashion of the olden time, meekly joined as if in prayer; while around it are displayed the helmet, coat of mail, gauntlets, shield, and sheath of the sword, that once gleamed so terrible in battle to hostile Frenchman and Spaniard. The inscription, in old French, tells us that:—" Here lieth the noble prince, the Lord Edward, eldest son of the very noble King Edward III., late Prince of

Aquitaine and Wales, Duke of Cornwall, and Earl of Chester, who died on Trinity Sunday, the 8th of June, in the year of grace, 1376. On whose soul God have mercy! Amen."

"The good fortune of England," says an old writer, " as if it had been inherent in his person, flourished in his health, languished in his sickness, and expired at his death, with whom died all the hope of Englishmen. During his life they feared no invasion of the enemy, nor encounter in battle; for he assailed no nation but he overcame, and besieged no city that he did not take."

It may give us some notion of the way in which our ancestors of five centuries ago viewed things, when we mention that it was commonly thought at the time, that the peculiar position of two planets, Saturn and Jupiter, had something to do with the prince's lamented death. But nobody doubted that a huge bearded comet (one with a tail perhaps as long as the glorious one of 1858), which was seen in the heavens the year preceding his decease, predicted it, if it did not actually cause it!

The captal, who was still ungenerously detained in prison at the time of the prince's death, did not long survive him. Grief for the loss of his master is said to have shortened the life of this gallant Englishman, who died in captivity. He might have had his liberty, had he been willing to take an oath never again to

bear arms against France. Death in prison was pref-
erable to liberty on such terms; and the name of
John de Greilly, Captal de Buch, ought to be had in
lasting honour by his countrymen, as patriot as well as
hero.

After the death of his renowned son, King Edward
retired, mourning and breaking his heart, to his palace
at Eltham where, in about a twelvemonth, he too died;
it is said, forlorn, friendless, forsaken by every one
save a priest, who, bending over the dying man, spoke
words of heavenly consolation in his ear, fast closing
to all earthly sounds. Humbly did the royal penitent
acknowledge his errors; and, with that mighty Name
upon his lips, which can alone assure sinful men of
pardon, for His sake Who bought it upon the bitter
cross, the great Edward yielded up his weary spirit.

Those splendid victories in France, which marked
the reign of King Edward and his heroic son, were like
a dream of conquest; for when his grey head was laid
low, by the side of loving Philippa, the last fragment of
them had disappeared, with the exception of Calais;
whose loss was destined to break the already more than
half-broken heart of one of his most unhappy successors.

The Princess of Wales, the once beautiful Joan, survived her lord for some years. She, too, was honoured
and loved by the English people. In one of the fierce
outbreaks of the citizens of London, the populace

sacrificed their murderous resentment against the Duke
of Lancaster (who had given them violent offence), to
her intercession; contenting themselves instead, with
hanging his coat-of-arms upside down in the streets, by
way of intimating that they considered him a dishon-
oured knight. And on another occasion she stood between him and the wrath of her son King Richard;
earning for herself the blessing bestowed upon the
"peacemakers," by painfully travelling from the one to
the other, until she had reconciled the two : thus avert-
ing the horrors of a civil war which was on the point
of arising out of their quarrel.

Not even her virtues and popularity, however, could
shield her from insult and violence at the hands of Wat
Tyler's vagabond host during their famous insurrection.
Marching upon London from Kent, they fell in with the
princess and her ladies returning from a pilgrimage to.
Canterbury,—one of the acts of piety of that day,—set
upon her carriage, treated herself with base insolence,
and after frightening them all almost out of their lives,
suffered them to make their escape to the Tower, where
they hoped to find safety with the king. But while he
went to meet the rebels at Mile End, the Tower was
surprised by others of them who had remained in
the city to do mischief. These wretches rushed hither
and thither, killing and slaying without mercy, broke
into the apartments of the princess, and smashed even
her bed, so that she was carried out fainting ; in which

state she was got away, by the river, to another of the king's palaces, where she remained, half dead with terror, until the insurrection was subdued, and the king himself hastened to comfort his mother with the good news. Her death, nine years after that of the prince, is said to have been caused by grief for the apprehended fate of her son, the Earl of Huntingdon (the son of her first husband), who having, in a fit of passion, killed Lord Ralph Stafford, was, spite of the pleadings of his mother, threatened with capital punishment for his crime : a doom which, however, he eventually escaped.

The Black Prince left but one child, a son, afterwards Richard II. Of his fate none can speak certainly, for the walls of Pontefract Castle still keep their melancholy secret. He died childless; so that, literally, in the "next generation," the "posterity" of the hero of Crecy and Poitiers was "destroyed," and "his name" "blotted out!"

"Deus judex est. Hunc humiliat, et hunc exaltat!"—Ps. lxxv.

BOOKS FOR BOYS.

BY R. M. BALLANTYNE.

Hudson Bay; or, Everyday Life in the Wilds of North America. With 46 Engravings. Crown 8vo, cloth extra. Price 5s.

The Young Fur-Traders. A Tale of the Far North. With Illustrations. Post 8vo, cloth. Price 3s. 6d.

Ungava. A Tale of Eskimo Land. With Illustrations. Post 8vo, cloth. Price 3s. 6d.

The Coral Island. A Tale of the Pacific. With Illustrations. Post 8vo, cloth. Price 3s. 6d.

Martin Rattler; or, A Boy's Adventures in the Forests of Brazil. With Illustrations. Post 8vo, cloth. Price 3s. 6d.

The Dog Crusoe and His Master. A Tale of the Western Prairies. With Illustrations. Post 8vo, cloth. Price 3s. 6d.

The Gorilla Hunters. A Tale of Western Africa. With Illustrations. Post 8vo, cloth. Price 3s. 6d.

The World of Ice; or, Adventures in the Polar Regions. With Engravings. Post 8vo, cloth. Price 3s. 6d.

The Ocean and its Wonders. With 60 Engravings. Post 8vo, cloth extra. Price 3s.

VOYAGES, TRAVEL, AND ADVENTURE.

The Eastern Archipelago. A Description of the Scenery, Animal and Vegetable Life, People, and Physical Wonders of the Islands in the Eastern Seas. By the Author of "The Arctic World," &c. With 60 Engravings and a Map. Crown 8vo, cloth extra. Price 5s.

The Lake Regions of Central Africa. A Record of Modern Discovery. By JOHN GEDDIE. With 32 Illustrations. Post 8vo, cloth extra. Price 3s. 6d.

Recent Polar Voyages. A Record of Adventure and Discovery from the Search after Franklin to the Voyage of the *Alert* and the *Discovery* (1875-76). With 62 Engravings. Crown 8vo, cloth. Price 5s.

Great Shipwrecks. A Record of Perils and Disasters at Sea—1544-1877. With 58 fine Engravings. Crown 8vo, cloth. Price 5s.

Kane's Arctic Explorations. The Second Grinnell Expedition in Search of Sir John Franklin. With 60 Engravings. Crown 8vo, cloth extra. Price 5s.

Pictures of Travel in Far-off Lands. A Companion to the Study of Geography.—CENTRAL AMERICA. With 50 Engravings. Post 8vo, cloth. Price 2s.

Pictures of Travel in Far-off Lands.—SOUTH AMERICA. With 50 Engravings. Post 8vo, cloth. Price 2s.

On the Nile. The Story of a Family Trip to the Land of Egypt. By SARA K. HUNT. With 16 Engravings. Post 8vo, cloth extra. 3s.

T. NELSON AND SONS, LONDON, EDINBURGH, AND NEW YORK.

BOOKS FOR BOYS.

BY THE LATE W. H. G. KINGSTON.

In the Wilds of Florida. With 37 Engravings. Gilt edges. Price 5s.

My First Voyage to Southern Seas. With 52 Engravings. Gilt edges. Price 5s.

Old Jack. A Sea Tale. With 66 Engravings. Gilt edges. Price 5s.

Saved from the Sea ; or, The Loss of the *Viper*, and the Adventures of her Crew in the Great Sahara. With 30 Full-page Engravings. Gilt edges. Price 5s.

The South Sea Whaler. A Story of the Loss of the *Champion*, and the Adventures of her Crew. With upwards of 30 Engravings. Gilt edges. Price 5s.

Twice Lost. A Story of Shipwreck, and of Adventure in the Wilds of Australia. With 36 Engravings. Gilt edges. Price 5s.

A Voyage Round the World. A Tale for Boys. With 42 Engravings. Gilt edges. Price 5s.

The Wanderers ; or, Adventures in the Wilds of Trinidad and up the Orinoco. With 30 Full-page Engravings. Gilt edges. Price 5s.

The Young Llanero. A Story of War and Wild Life in Venezuela. With 44 Engravings. Gilt edges. Price 5s.

The Young Rajah. A Story of Indian Life and Adventure. With upwards of 40 Full-page Engravings. Gilt edges. Price 5s.

In the Eastern Seas ; or, The Regions of the Bird of Paradise. A Tale for Boys. With 111 Illustrations. Crown 8vo, gilt edges. 6s.

In the Wilds of Africa. With upwards of 70 Illustrations. Crown 8vo, gilt edges. Price 6s.

Afar in the Forest. With 41 Full-page Engravings. Cloth extra. Price 3s. 6d.

In the Rocky Mountains. A Tale of Adventure. With 41 Engravings. Price 3s. 6d.

In New Granada ; or, Heroes and Patriots. With 36 Full-page Engravings. Price 3s. 6d.

Stories of the Sagacity of Animals. With 60 Illustrations by HARRISON WEIR. Price 3s. 6d.

Almost a Hero ; or, School Days at Ashcombe. By ROBERT RICHARDSON, Author of "Ralph's Year in Russia," "The Young Cragsman," &c. With 7 Engravings. Post 8vo, cloth extra. Price 3s. 6d.

Odd Moments of the Willoughby Boys. By EMILY HARTLEY. Post 8vo, cloth extra. Price 2s. 6d.

Culm Rock ; or, Ready Work for Willing Hands. A Book for Boys. By J. W. BRADLEY. Foolscap 8vo, cloth extra. Price 2s.

The Boy's Country Book. By WILLIAM HOWITT. Post 8vo, cloth. With Illustrations. Price 3s. 6d.

> *From "Edinburgh Review," July 1879.*—"To our mind William Howitt's 'Boy's Country Book' is the best of the kind that has ever been written."

Nuts for Boys to Crack. By the Rev. JOHN TODD, D.D., Author of "Simple Sketches," &c. Royal 18mo. Price 1s. 6d.

T. NELSON AND SONS, LONDON, EDINBURGH, AND NEW YORK.

ILLUSTRATED BOOKS OF SCIENCE AND HISTORY.

Rambles in Rome. An Archæological and Historical Guide to the Museums, Galleries, Villas, Churches, and Antiquities of Rome and the Campagna. By S. RUSSELL FORBES, Archæological and Historical Lecturer on Roman Antiquities. With Maps, Plans, and Illustrations. Post 8vo, cloth extra. Price 3s. 6d.

Pompeii and Herculaneum, the Buried Cities of Campania: Their History, their Destruction, and their Remains. By W. H. DAVENPORT ADAMS. With 57 Engravings and a Plan of Pompeii. Post 8vo, cloth extra. Price 3s. 6d.

The Land of the Nile; or, Egypt, Past and Present. By the Author of "The Mediterranean Illustrated." With upwards of 100 Engravings. Post 8vo. Price 3s. 6d.

Maury's Physical Geography of the Sea. With 13 Charts printed in Colours. 8vo. Price 5s.

Merchant Enterprise; or, Pictures of the History of Commerce from the Earliest Times. By J. HAMILTON FYFE. With 10 Illustrations. Post 8vo, cloth extra. Price 3s. 6d.

Lighthouses and Lightships: A Descriptive and Historical Account of their Mode of Construction and Organization. With 70 Illustrations from Photographs and other sources. Post 8vo, cloth extra. Price 3s. 6d.

Triumphs of Invention and Discovery in Science and Art. With Illustrations. Post 8vo, cloth extra. Price 2s. 6d.

Wonders of the Physical World—The Glacier, Iceberg, Icefield, and Avalanche. By W. H. DAVENPORT ADAMS. With 75 Engravings. Post 8vo, cloth extra. Price 3s. 6d.

BOOKS BY MRS. SURR.

Stories about Dogs. By Mrs. SURR. With 12 Tinted Engravings by HARRISON WEIR. 4to, cloth extra. Price 3s. 6d.

Stories about Cats. By Mrs. SURR. With 12 Tinted Engravings by HARRISON WEIR, and other Artists. 4to, cloth extra. Price 3s. 6d.

Good out of Evil. A Tale for Children. By Mrs. SURR, Author of "Sea Birds and the Story of their Lives," &c. With 32 Illustrations by GIACOMELLI. Foolscap 8vo, gilt edges. Price 2s.

Sea Birds and the Lessons of their Lives. By Mrs. SURR, Author of "Good out of Evil." With 24 Illustrations by GIACOMELLI and other Artists. Post 8vo, cloth, gilt edges. Price 2s.

MRS. SURR'S PICTURE BOOKS FOR CHILDREN.

Price One Shilling each.

Each with Six Illustrations printed in Colours in the highest style of the Art.

Birds and their Nests. Drawn by GIACOMELLI, and Described by Mrs. SURR.

Bird Pictures. Drawn by GIACOMELLI, and Described by Mrs. SURR.

Animals and Birds of the Bible. With Six Pages of Beautifully Coloured Engravings. The descriptive Letterpress by Mrs. SURR. 4to. Pictorial Cover.

T. NELSON AND SONS, LONDON, EDINBURGH, AND NEW YORK.

STORY BOOKS OF NATURAL HISTORY,

RICHLY ILLUSTRATED.

Jenny and the Insects; or, Little Toilers and their Industries. With 26 Illustrations by GIACOMELLI. Post 8vo, cloth extra, gilt edges. Price 3s. 6d.

Tiny Workers; or, Man's Little Rivals in the Animal World. With 13 Engravings. Price 1s. 6d.

The History of the Robins. By Mrs. TRIMMER. Illustrated with 16 Original Drawings by GIACOMELLI, engraved by Rouget, Berveiller, Whymper, Sargent, &c. *New and Cheaper Edition.* Post 8vo, gilt edges. Price 3s.

In the Woods. By M. K. M., Author of "The Birds We See," &c. With 34 Illustrations by GIACOMELLI. Post 8vo, cloth extra. Price 2s. 6d.

Sea Birds, and the Lessons of their Lives. By Mrs. SURR. With 24 Engravings. Foolscap 8vo, cloth, gilt edges. Price 2s.

Stories of the Dog, and his Cousins the Wolf, the Jackal, and the Hyena. With Stories Illustrating their Place in the Animal World. By Mrs. HUGH MILLER. With 34 Engravings. Foolscap 8vo, cloth. Price 1s. 6d.

Stories of the Cat, and her Cousins the Lion, the Tiger, and the Leopard. With Stories Illustrating their Place in the Animal World. By Mrs. HUGH MILLER. With 29 Engravings. Foolscap 8vo, cloth. Price 1s. 6d.

Talks with Uncle Richard about Wild Animals. By Mrs. GEORGE CUPPLES. With 75 Illustrations. 18mo, cloth. 1s. 6d.

Mamma's Stories about Domestic Pets. By Mrs. GEORGE CUPPLES. With 56 Illustrations. 18mo, cloth. Price 1s. 6d.

Things in the Forest. By MARY and ELIZABETH KIRBY. With Coloured Frontispiece, and 50 Illustrations. Royal 18mo, cloth. Price 1s. 6d.

Stories about Dogs. By Mrs. SURR. With 12 Tinted Engravings by HARRISON WEIR. 4to, cloth extra. Price 3s. 6d.

Stories about Cats. By Mrs. SURR. With 12 Tinted Engravings by HARRISON WEIR, and other Artists. 4to, cloth extra. Price 3s. 6d.

History of Good Dog Fanny and Tuft the Canary. With other Stories, all true. By Mrs. GASKELL, of Ingersley. Price 1s. 6d.

T. NELSON AND SONS, LONDON, EDINBURGH, AND NEW YORK.

NEW SERIES OF EIGHTEENPENNY BOOKS.

Story of the Beacon Fire ; or, Trust in God and Do the Right. By NAOMI. Post 8vo, cloth.

May's Sixpence ; or, Waste Not, Want Not. A Tale. By M. A. PAULL, Author of "Tim's Troubles," &c. Royal 18mo.

Willie's Choice; or, All is not Gold that Glitters. By M. A. PAULL. Post 8vo.

Roe Carson's Enemy; or, The Struggle for Self-Conquest. By the Rev. E. N. HOARE, M.A., Rector of Acrise, Kent, Author of "Harvey Compton's Holiday," &c. Royal 18mo.

Tempered Steel ; or, Tried in the Fire. By the Rev. E. N. HOARE, M.A., Author of "Roe Carson's Enemy," &c. Foolscap 8vo, cloth.

Working in the Shade ; or, Lowly Sowing brings Glorious Reaping. By the Rev. T. P. WILSON, M.A., Author of "True to His Colours," &c. Royal 18mo.

Little Hazel, the King's Messenger. By the Author of "Little Snowdrop and her Golden Casket," &c. Post 8vo.

The Crown of Glory; or, "Faithful unto Death." A Scottish Story of Martyr Times. By the Author of "Little Hazel, the King's Messenger." Post 8vo, cloth.

The Guiding Pillar. A Story for the Young. By the Author of "Under the Old Oaks; or, Won by Love." Foolscap 8vo.

Little Snowdrop and her Golden Casket. By the Author of "Little Hazel, the King's Messenger," &c. Post 8vo.

Under the Old Oaks ; or, Won by Love. By the Author of "Little Hazel, the King's Messenger," &c. Post 8vo.

Breakers Ahead ; or, Uncle Jack's Stories of Great Shipwrecks of Recent Times. By Mrs. SAXBY, Author of "Rock Bound," "Stories of Shetland," &c. Post 8vo, cloth.

Little Lily's Travels. A Book for the Young. With numerous Engravings. Post 8vo.

Aunt Martha's Corner Cupboard. A Story for Little Boys and Girls. By MARY and ELIZABETH KIRBY. With numerous Engravings. Post 8vo.

The Basket of Flowers. A Tale for the Young. With numerous Engravings. Post 8vo.

T. NELSON AND SONS, LONDON, EDINBURGH, AND NEW YORK.

INSTRUCTIVE BOOKS FOR THE YOUNG.

Eighteenpence each.

Brother Reginald's Golden Secret. By the Author of "Hope On," &c. Coloured Frontispiece and numerous Engravings. Royal 18mo.

Bunyan's Pilgrim's Progress. Royal 18mo.

Father's Coming Home. A Tale. By the Author of "Under the Microscope." Royal 18mo.

The Fisherman's Children ; or, The Sunbeam of Hardrick Cove. With Coloured Frontispiece and 26 Engravings. Royal 18mo.

Grandpapa's Keepsakes ; or, Take Heed will Surely Speed. By Mrs. GEORGE CUPPLES. With Coloured Frontispiece and Vignette, and 45 Engravings. Royal 18mo.

The Fisherman's Boy ; or, "All have not the same Gifts." With Coloured Frontispiece. Royal 18mo.

King Jack of Haylands. With Coloured Frontispiece and numerous Engravings. Royal 18mo.

Lessons on the Life of Christ for the Little Ones at Home. By the Author of "Hymns from the Land of Luther." With Coloured Frontispiece and 30 Engravings. Royal 18mo.

Simple Sketches. By the Rev. JOHN TODD, D.D., Author of "The Student's Guide," &c. Illustrated. Royal 18mo.

Under the Microscope ; or, "Thou Shalt Call Me My Father." By the Author of "Village Missionaries." With Coloured Frontispiece and 17 Engravings. Royal 18mo.

Stories from the History of the Jews. From the Babylonish Captivity to the Fall of Jerusalem. By A. L. O. E. With Coloured Frontispiece and Vignette, and 30 Illustrations. Royal 18mo.

The Story of a Needle. By A. L. O. E. Illustrated. Royal 18mo.

Watch—Work—Wait. A Story of the Battle of Life. By SARAH MYERS. Royal 18mo.

Susy's Flowers ; or, "Blessed are the Merciful, for They shall obtain Mercy." By the Author of "Hope On," &c. With Coloured Frontispiece and Vignette, and numerous Engravings. Royal 18mo.

Sweetest when Crushed ; or, The Blessing of Trials when Rightly Borne. A Tale for the Young. By AGNES VEITCH. Royal 18mo.

Things in the Forest. By MARY and ELIZABETH KIRBY. With Coloured Frontispiece and 50 Illustrations. Royal 18mo.

Wings and Stings. By A. L. O. E. With Coloured Frontispiece and 16 Engravings. Royal 18mo.

The Swedish Twins. A Tale for the Young. By the Author of "The Babes in the Basket." With Coloured Frontispiece. Royal 18mo.

The Boy Artist. A Tale by the Author of "Hope On." With Coloured Frontispiece and numerous Engravings. Royal 18mo.

Little Aggie's Fresh Snowdrops, and what they did in One Day. With Coloured Frontispiece and 30 Engravings. Royal 18mo.

Wonders of the Heavens—The Stars, including an Account of Nebulæ, Comets, and Meteors. With 50 Engravings. Royal 18mo.

Wonders of the Heavens—The Sun, Moon, and Planets. Their Physical Character, Appearance, and Phenomena. With 46 Engravings. Royal 18mo.

T. NELSON AND SONS, LONDON, EDINBURGH, AND NEW YORK.

NEW SERIES OF SHILLING BOOKS.

The Search for Franklin. With Engravings from Designs by the Artist of the Expedition. Foolscap 8vo.

The Rocket; or, The Story of the Stephensons, Father and Son. By H. C. KNIGHT. Illustrated. Foolscap 8vo.

No Gains without Pains; or, The Story of Samuel Budgett, the Successful Merchant. By H. C. KNIGHT. Foolscap 8vo.

Truth and its Triumph; or, The Story of the Jewish Twins. By Mrs. SARAH S. BAKER, Author of "The Children on the Plains." Foolscap 8vo.

Trots' Letters to her Doll. By MARY E. BROOMFIELD, Author of "Daddy Dick," &c. Foolscap 8vo.

NEW SERIES OF NINEPENNY BOOKS.

BY MRS. GEORGE CUPPLES.

Each with Coloured Frontispiece, an Illuminated Side, and Numerous Engravings. 18mo.

Bertha Marchmont; or, All is not Gold that Glitters.
Fanny Silvester; or, A Merry Heart doeth Good like a Medicine.
Bluff Crag; or, A Good Word Costs Nothing.
Hugh Wellwood's Success; or, Where there's a Will there's a Way.
Alice Leighton; or, A Good Name is rather to be Chosen than Riches.
Carry's Rose; or, The Magic of Kindness.
Little May and her Friend Conscience. By M. PARROTT.

These are bright, cheerful stories, having for their object the inculcation of the principle implied in the second title of the books. They are profusely illustrated, prettily bound, and make most attractive presents for children.

NEW SERIES OF SIXPENNY BOOKS.

18mo, cloth.

Each with Frontispiece Printed in Oil Colours.

Amy Harrison; or, Heavenly Seed and Heavenly Dew.
Dreaming Susy, and other Stories.
A Mother's Blessing, and other Stories.
Children of the Kingdom, and other Stories.
The Old Castle, and other Stories.
Little Cross-Bearers, and other Stories.

T. NELSON AND SONS, LONDON, EDINBURGH, AND NEW YORK.

www.ingramcontent.com/pod-product-compliance
Lightning Source LLC
Chambersburg PA
CBHW021051030726
47496CB00006B/1780